JOE FURY AND THE HARD DEATH

To Denis +
Carl

JOE FURY AND THE HARD DEATH

Paul Anthony Long

FrontList Books

Published by FrontList Books.
An imprint of Soft Editions Ltd,
Gullane, East Lothian, Scotland.

A catalogue record for this book is
available from the British Library.

ISBN: 1-84350-105-8

ISBN 13: 9781843501053

To my mum, for putting up with this kind of madness as I was growing up.

ONE

The diner sits in the middle of the vast, empty desert, only one road nailing it to anywhere at all. It's a small, squat joint with a layer of dust on every surface, but it's the only place I can meet my contact.

Preston walks out wearing a dress as part of his disguise. It suits him. The wig could do with some adjusting but you can't have everything.

'New car?' He nods at the shark parked up against the tumbleweed, and I nod. 'Nice.'

'What's the problem?' I sip the coffee and settle down to business. Preston slides into the seat opposite and drops a pamphlet on the table. It's nothing special. A package. Inside a publicity photo—all teeth and eyes—and a very large sum of money.

'Kieran Walsh. We want him back to face charges.'

'What did he do?'

'Nothing you need to know about. We need him back.'

'Destination?'

'We don't know. The last we heard he was at the end of this road.' Preston scratches his wig and looks strangely comfortable.

'Give me a week.' I tell him.

'You've got a day.' He gets up and adjusts his skirt. 'Blueberry pie?'

'Not at my age.'

Just then the door bursts open. It's trouble.

TWO

She looks young and out of breath and I can tell the first thing she'll do is make a beeline for me. But I'm wrong. She heads straight for the back exit.

Preston watches her like a hawk. She disappears and he wanders off behind the counter and into the kitchen. I hear a clatter, a clang, and then the trouble's back in the room.

She creeps towards the window and looks out. Nothing but empty wasteland. In the end she notices me.

'If you take the last turn at the end of the road you'll end

up in a coffin. Mark my words and mark them well, Joe.'
She looks serious, and without a scent of derangement. Which
makes her even more dangerous.

'My name's not Joe,' I tell her.

'It is now.'

A flurry of noise at the diner door and a troupe of nuns—
four of them—walk in, wimpled up to the eyeballs. They're
packing.

'Trouble.' She doesn't need to tell me. 'For now I'm Suzanne,' says the trouble and slips into the booth opposite me.
'You got a cannon?'

'I'm a pacifist,' I lie. 'It's against my principles.'

'Waitress.' The nun with the biggest wimple hammers the
table and Preston walks out. 'We're looking for the widow's
peak. The man with the rudimentary sense of perception told
us you knew the way.'

Preston looks stumped. I guess nuns weren't in his game
plan. 'Try the chilli.'

'It's against my religion,' says the biggest nun, and then
they get serious.

The robes burst open and a legion of weapons slams straight
into my face. I hit the floor, dragging Sue with me, and she's
already got an Uzi in her fist.

She peals off a burst under the table and takes out the legs
of the nearest penguin. Before the woman has time to hit the
ground, Sue's up like a jack-in-the-box and the Uzi's tearing
the face off the next nun.

'Back exit,' she shouts, but Preston's out with a cannon
pointing straight in our direction.

'Down, pooch,' he says. Sue spares him a glance, and then
stops the Uzi talking.

THREE

'Straight out of the gutter.' Preston's not an eloquent man. He
walks around the counter with the cannon aiming slap bang
between Sue's eyes. 'Wondered how long before you turned
up.'

'Drop the hot air, Preston,' she says. 'You let this muppet
know what he's in for?'

'She one of us or one of them?' I ask Preston, but the point is moot because the grenade that was in my hand is rolling across the floor.

'She's one of Kieran's briefs,' says Preston, and then his eyes go wide as the pineapple trickles towards the feet of the terrified nuns.

'It's got a ten second fuse,' I tell him, and then me and the trouble are racing for the back door and we're out in the fresh air. Before we can dive for the car the building goes up. And we're stuck in the middle of the explosion.

FOUR

This is definitely Armageddon. Not what it feels like but what it actually is. Fireballs, pitchforks, the wasted dead on every side of you. Nothing but the searing stain of your own flesh burning a hole in your reason. And when the pain gets too much you can't even breathe for the effort, because the mercy that would give would cancel out the degradation you find yourself steeped in.

Or else it would be, but the fireball is swift and fast and me and Sue hit the ground and keep running. Behind us the window of the diner blows out with a million shards of fury and the nuns are screaming.

Spare shells are popping off as we get to the car and I'm in and we're off before the door bursts open and something— something like Preston in a blazing wig—is out there and pointing a gun at us. But he's swallowed by the ball of dust kicked up by the back tyres and we're fishtailing down the endless highway stretching out into the cracked, gasping desert ahead of us.

'We died back there,' says Sue. And she's right.

FIVE

'We died but we're back here now, so it's not worth thinking too hard about,' I tell her, because I know by looking at her she's the inquisitive type. 'Just leave it for now and you'll get your answers. And right now I need some. I want everything you know in here.' I tap the side of my head and she looks at me with these deep, judgemental reptilian eyes, and I know she's looking right inside of me. It doesn't shake me.

'Kieran's whatever you want him to be,' she tells me, and even if it's nothing but hot air there's conviction in her eyes. 'Preston and Kieran used to be lovers because that's what Preston wanted. Kieran gives you a belief system and that's why people want him dead, because he shares what he's got with everyone, and for everyone it's something different. A different life, a different zone, a different way of thinking, of being, of believing—it doesn't matter. It's different for everyone and we all come away scarred. Some of us learn to live with it and some of us don't, and because Kieran keeps living, some people want him dead or trapped. He's too dangerous.'

'Sounds like a wimp.'

'You never had a belief?'

'Not something anyone could do anything about.'

'See, that's where you're wrong,' she says.

'I'm a man who has everything, honey,' I tell her. 'My car, some smokes, and a good glass of bourbon to drink. You don't need much more than that in life.'

'Then you don't need him, which makes you a threat.'

'You're just flapping now,' I tell her, and she knows I'm right. 'Tell me the rest. Tell me about the nuns.'

'So you do want something.'

The brakes go on. The car squeals to a halt. I pop the door open and look at her.

'You can walk or talk. It's your call.'

'Kieran's got a family,' she says, and nods to the road ahead. 'They're right there.'

SIX

It's like a barrier. A motor home stretched across the highway. A man sits on the roof in a deckchair, shades on the end of his fat nose, a beer in one hand and a stubby pump action shotgun across his lap.

'You're a long way from home, boy,' says the man, and I pop the glove compartment open and pull out some bourbon. The man is a living cliché. A puppet.

'Who's pulling the strings, Sue?'

'You are.'

'Ditch the metaphysical mumbo jumbo and tell me what's going on. We had an empty road.'

She nods to the surrounding bleakness. 'You want mountains and they'll appear.' And bang—she's right. A long way off, but on the horizon sits a string of mountains that wasn't there before.

I take a shot from the bottle and pass it to Sue. She hits and doesn't choke.

'I'm not even asking where they came from.' I flick an eye at the mountain range. Then I look at the motor home. 'That yours?'

'Trust me, Joe, I didn't make a thing happen which you didn't want to.' She looks convincing, but it doesn't wash with me.

'I knew you were trouble,' I say, then flick the car into gear and take a lazy detour around the motor home. The man doesn't look up—just waves a friendly goodbye and then passes into history.

'You want to know about belief?' I ask. Sue nods.

SEVEN

The shunt from behind puts an end to my words. The motor home is in for the kill and the driver has the look of the devil in his eye.

'Unfriendly family,' I say to Sue, then gun the engine and the shark starts to gain space from the motor home.

'Once you meet Kieran we all become part of his family.' Sue sounds like a wingnut but her eyes lack the gleam of the zealot. It's not a comfortable feeling.

The motor home engine grumbles and roars like something deep and primitive, and the machine surges forward and eats up the distance.

'If you're willing to use the Uzi on the nuns,' I tell Sue, 'you can use it on the tyres. Take them out.'

She spins in her seat and aims low for the tyres. The motor home leaps towards us and closes in for the kill. The Uzi spits a hail of fire and tears up the front of the vehicle as it crashes into the back of us. The shark fishtails, laying a trail of smoke

11

across the tarmac, and before we know it we're off the road and sliding to a stop.

Motor home man is out before we can react. But no shotgun. Instead he runs for us, dragging something big and human, but unmoving, behind him. I turn to gun the engine, which squeals and churns in protest, and then stamp on the gas and we're off again.

When I glance in the rear view the man is in the back. He's got a corpse with him. Both of them are smiling.

'Don't worry,' says the man, nodding at the corpse. 'He's not the dead one.' Then he jams a tazer to his throat and his mouth and eyes light up with blue fire and he's gone—dead—smoke rolling lazily up from his hair.

Immediately the corpse next to him jerks upright.

'Morning,' says the corpse. 'Just call me Ishmael.'

EIGHT

'It's not the dead you have to worry about,' says Ishmael as he stretches and groans. 'It's more of the same old living crap that really puts the greaser in my whisky.' He pops a shoulder and sighs. 'Bourbon. I know you've got it.'

I turn to Sue. 'The family.'

'We're all family, Kemo Sabe,' says Ishmael. 'I know everything about you, Joe. Even your real name. And Kieran wants a meet.'

'Good,' I say. 'Let's cut to the end of this chase. I've been paid.'

'Let's play a game first,' says Ishmael. 'A game of—' But the words are frozen in his mouth because the snout of my gun is resting between his eyes.

'No games, Ishmael.' I stare at him in the rear view, one hand on the wheel and one on the gun jammed right up to his head. 'He wants to meet me—I want to meet him. Where is he?'

'Take a left turn.' For a dead man he seems pretty scared.

There is no turning in the road. But I turn anyway.

And everything changes.

NINE

Now I understand the concept of Nirvana. It's like a dream come true. Beauty and majesty all wrapped into a bowl of perfection. Not a trace of falsehood or misunderstanding. Not a strand wrong in the perfect reality of where I am. Not a façade out of place.

Downtown. Dark. Neon. Alleyways. Huddled figures. Hats and smoke.

The brakes go on.

'You can smile.' Ishmael nods at me in the rear view, and that breaks the spell. I snap around.

'Hypnosis,' I say. 'Let it drop.'

'Step out,' suggests Ishmael. 'Test the water for yourself.'

'If it was perfect I wouldn't need to smile,' I tell him. I push back his head with the barrel of my gun and the look of conviction starts to drop from his weathered face. 'Now back to reality.'

'We're stuck,' offers Ishmael.

'There has to be another way out.'

He snatches a worried look around. 'I have a story. A short one. A man who wanted death the most in the world was forced to trade his dream for a brother, and when the brother died they both wound up in eternity. Who am I?'

'An asshole,' I mutter, and step out of the car.

TEN

The ground is solid. Inside it's smoky and dark. The corners are full of shadows. To my right stands a neon-lit bar. That's where I head.

'Whisky. Neat.'

The barman serves me and I knock it down. The door opens and Sue's there with the Uzi in her hand, Ishmael trailing behind her like a dog, dragging his corpse with him.

'This is exactly what Kieran wants,' she says as she takes a seat next to me and nods for a short. 'This is what you believe in and Kieran's bringing it to you.'

'It's better than a sock in the jaw.' I nestle back another whisky and let the drink clear my head.

'You've got to break out of this fugue, Joe.' She's starting to give me a headache with her whining. Over in the corner a smoky brunette sits with her head in the shadows and a smile on her lips. I take a step towards her.

Sue stops me. Hand on the arm. Warning stare. She shakes her head and she's right. Kieran's doing something to my mind.

I grab Ishmael and shove him up against the bar.

'Okay, dead man, start talking. What's going on?'

'I don't want to play anymore.' Ishmael tasers his brother who twitches like a live wire and suddenly Ishmael's down on the ground and his brother's on his feet.

'Look at her, Joe,' says Ishmael's brother nodding to the brunette, and I can't help looking. 'She's probably got a stack of money, a heavy rack and a tough case for you. You want to give this all up for a lost cause like Preston's folly?'

'Cut the wise talk.' I slam Ishmael's brother back. 'Tell me the story.'

'She knows.' He nods at Sue and all eyes turn to her. She doesn't look easy.

'Right now you're the one spilling tomorrow's headlines. Now speak.' I shove him again and he knows I mean business.

'Kieran just wants to trade. Nothing special. You get all this for his peace of mind and the ability to leave the case behind.'

'Too bad, delivery boy,' I tell him. 'I've already been paid.'

'Preston tried to kill you.'

'A technicality.' I shrug it off. 'And besides, it wasn't me he wanted. It's the trouble he's after.' I nod to Sue. 'And right now she's with me.'

'Don't do it, Joe,' says Ishmael's brother. 'There's hard times ahead.'

'There's hard times here,' I snarl, and let him drop. I nod to Sue. 'Let's blow this pop stand.'

'She hasn't told you, has she?' Ishmael's brother has a smile on his face that I don't like the look of. 'She hasn't told you about what she did for Kieran.'

I turn to him. 'And?'

'I'll take you there.'

ELEVEN

Flashback to some forgotten time in a forgotten place. There's bombs and guns and mess and the whole thing is punctured through with the stench of death and panic and screams and decay. The trouble's gone, but Ishmael and his brother are both alive, both dressed in khaki, and both aware of the situation.

'What's the deal?' Bullets whiz over my head as I light up a cigar and wait for the story.

Ishmael's brother holds out his hand for me to shake. 'I'm Dougie.' I ignore him.

'We're right in the middle of a war, Joe,' says Ishmael. 'That mean anything to you?'

'It means you're in danger of eating my fist, Ahab—now what's going on?'

'You pick a conflict and I'll tell you what it is.'

I don't have time for this but I look around anyway. A lot of carbines and dead bodies. A shell whistles down and blows a chunk of mud and gore twenty feet to my left, and Ishmael and Dougie duck.

'Second world war.'

'Could be.' Dougie shrugs. 'Might be anywhere. Vietnam. Iraq, Iran, Afghanistan, Kosovo, the Congo—it doesn't matter. This is the scene of an endless war. It's where every battle that ever happened is being played out second by second. Suzanne is part of that progress and so is Kieran. This is what people want. The money shot.'

'You're making about as much sense as my ex-wife,' I tell them. 'What's this got to do with Sue?'

'She's not real. She's a figment of Kieran's imagination. She was made up to seduce you.'

'Then why the war?'

'She *is* the war,' screams Ishmael as an M50 roars a few feet away and a phalanx of Zulu warriors storm over the churned up, twisted corpses of a thousand dead. Just then a bullet slams into Dougie's head and tears a huge chuck out of his skull. He collapses sideways in a pool of his own blood and brains. Ishmael looks nonplussed.

'Oh dear,' he says in a very quiet voice. 'That's torn it. We're stuck here now.'

TWELVE

By the third time I slug him he's had enough.

'Hey, it's bad news about your brother but I didn't ask to be dragged into this mess.'

'There's another option,' pleads Ishmael. 'My brother was the connection and now that connection is broken. Look over the ridge.'

I do. Nothing but blood and pain for miles in every direction.

'Small shack right in the middle. See it?' And Ishmael's right. It's a shadow against the cannon smoke and the raging fires, but it's there alright.

'Time for some action.'

I'm over the ridge and racing for the nearest foxhole before Ishmael has time to breathe. The bullets are churning up the ground around me, bombs blowing mud and body parts high into the air, the smell of cordite, blood, and choking acrid smoke. When I hit the foxhole there's a Tommy in there with a woman. I recognise her instantly. Felicia Browne.

'A long way from home,' I comment, and she spares me a momentary glance before popping a shot off at random. After all, the enemy is everywhere.

'It's not exactly the Spanish Civil War,' she mutters. An armour plated knight, screaming fury and death, breaches the foxhole. My right hook glances off the breast plate and Felicia wraps him in a leg lock and spins him onto his back. Before he's got time to move she slams six inches of bayonet into his throat, between helmet and breast plate, and he chokes his last in a mist of blood.

'Thanks, sister,' I mutter. 'I owe you.'

Ishmael hits the foxhole. Somehow he's got his hands on an MP40 and a face full of blood.

'Question,' I say, and he turns his crazed eyes to me. 'If Dougie's dead anyway then how can he die?' I spark up a match on the breast plate of the soldier Felicia iced and fume up another cheroot.

'He'll be back,' gasps Ishmael. 'Back on the road. Back where we shouldn't be with Suzanne and Kieran, and Kieran wants this and this isn't how it's supposed to be.'

'Tell me about it,' I say, and then we're up and out and pounding through the wilderness. I blind side a Maori with a spear and pole-axe a madman with a bolt action rifle, and we're knee deep in mud in the next foxhole. A shell hits nearby and somebody's head falls into my lap.

'This wasn't in the brochure.' I grab Ishmael and drag him close. By now we're eye to eye. His mind's gone. If it was ever there.

'Start talking, Ishmael. One minute we're on the road and now we're here. What the hell's going on.'

'*It's him!*' he says with emphasis, and something tells me logic's taken a back seat.

Then we're up and out once more and tearing up the distance. The cottage is almost in plain sight when the monk nails me good and square.

THIRTEEN

'Bless you, my son,' he sparks before I take his legs out. I'm just about to cold cock him when he holds up his hands for mercy.

'You're not one of them,' he bleats. I look around. Ishmael's a distant shadow racing for the cottage.

'You have any idea what's going on around here?'

'You've met the nuns,' says the monk. 'You know what they can do.'

'Don't tell me the penguins set this little ringer up?'

'The Sisters of the Immaculate Immolation aren't responsible. The man you seek is Kieran.'

'Tell me about it.' I was starting to get tired of hearing about this joker. 'You another acolyte or just here for the view?'

'Take this.' He thrusts a watch into my hand. 'Keep it over your heart. It will come in handy when the time is right.'

'Cut the crap, brother. I don't play that game.'

I stuff the watch back into the monk's pocket and leave him genuflecting in the mud as the cottage looms up in the distance. Only then I realise Ishmael's aiming the MP40 over my shoulder, his eyes wide with fear.

FOURTEEN

The sub-machine gun talks and I hit the dirt.

'Facking hell, mate, leave it out.'

It's the Tommy and he's not looking pleased.

'Drop the popgun, Ahab.' Ishmael lowers it but keeps it ready.

The Tommy runs up and hunches down by the wall, keeping an eye out. Bullets rake a line over his head and he ducks down further.

'Facking huns have got the place tied up. Tossers.'

I reach into my pocket for another cigar and feel something solid. It's the watch. The monk must have palmed it on me when I made a break for it.

'Nice watch, mate,' says the Tommy.

'Never trust a monk,' I say, and then realise my wallet's gone as well. 'They've got sticky fingers. And not just for the choirboys.'

'Talk later, fight now,' snaps Ishmael, and lets off a hail of leaden death at the shadows in the smoke. He raps three times on the cottage door. A moment of tension and the door slowly opens, revealing only blackness.

FIFTEEN

A match flares in the dark and I find the face of an old man looking down at me. The match lights a candle and suddenly we're in a living room. And it's quiet. And comfy.

Outside the windows the battle rages. Inside it's like a tomb.

'Cup of tea, mate?' It's the Tommy, and he's already making himself at home, snapping on the overhead lights and settling down on the biggest looking chair.

'I know you and you,' says the old man, pointing to the Tommy and Ishmael. 'But you . . .' He takes a step closer and squints at me. 'You're different. You're a phenomenon.'

'I'm all kinds of things, old timer,' I tell him. 'And right now I need to get back to my job.'

'Tish and phipsy.' The old man shakes his head. 'Come and have a cup of rosy.'

'No thanks, old man,' I say. 'I need closure.'

'We need to get to the machine,' says Ishmael. The old man waves him away and starts off out of the room.

'All in good time,' he says, and then he's gone.

'Okay, Ahab, where's the exit?' Ishmael nods to a door. 'And then what?'

'Then we get back.' Ishmael starts towards the door as the old man pipes up behind us.

'I wouldn't do that if I were you.' We turn and there he stands, a cup of tea in one hand and a rocket launcher in the other. 'Sugar?'

SIXTEEN

'See, the way I see it, we're sort of stuck in this eternal conflict because of the sins of man,' says the Tommy, munching on a biscuit and sipping his tea. 'It's like, the facking duality of nature to constantly be at war with oneself and yet yearn for peace, which, paradoxically, can only be brought about by the war we all yearn to bring an end to. See what I mean?'

The urge to slap him till he squeals is pretty strong at this moment, but I take a look at the old man. The rocket launcher's on the floor but the smile on his face tells me he's taking no crap today.

'And what do you think, young man?' He's talking to Ishmael.

Ishmael doesn't look happy. 'Erm ... Well, that's a good question when you consider the facts. After all, some people might say the very fact of war is a necessity against a political and social world status. Or country status. Uh ...'

He's flagging. The old man narrows his eyes and I can see his hand reaching for the rocket launcher.

'But then it's also a state of mind as much as a state of reality.' It doesn't mean anything but it seems to put the cooler on the old man. He smiles.

'Interesting. Random, but interesting.' The old man turns to me. 'And what about you?'

'Cut the chatter, old man,' I say as I whip out the popgun and aim for his forehead. 'Now make with the machine or your jawbone goes west.'

The old man smiles. Then sips his tea.

'We're civilised, Mr ...?'

'My name doesn't matter,' I snap. 'Finding a way out of this hell hole does.'

'But what's your philosophy on warfare?'

'Come on, Ahab.' I spare Ishmael a glance. 'Let's get out of here.'

Suddenly the wall behind the old man disappears and I see nothing but light.

SEVENTEEN

The rest of the walls fall down and we're on a stage facing a bank of lights. The old man's in a tux and some Chinese guy with a glittery suit stands behind him, a microphone in his hand and a grin on his face as wide as his collars. And what's worse, my gun is gone.

'I'm afraid that's the wrong answer,' says the old man, and the voice of God speaks.

'Welcome once again to this week's edition of "Morality".' It's big and it's booming and it's coming from everywhere. Canned applause fills the stage.

I glance around. The battlefield has gone. Instead we're in a giant, cavernous studio with an audience of cardboard cut-outs. It's like the living room has been transported slap bang into the middle of a game show.

'Ahab? What's the beef?'

Ishmael just shakes his head and looks worried.

'And please welcome your host for the evening, Sun Tzu!' the voice booms, and the Chinese guy walks down towards us.

'Thang you very much,' mutters Tzu. 'Tonight we'll be playing for the very existence of this man's soul.' And he's pointing at me.

'First of all,' slimes the old guy as he oils his way towards me, 'we have some questions.'

'Hey, Tzu?' I shout. 'Art of War not selling too good these days or this just your day job?'

'Your tactics are weak and foolish gumshoe,' he says in a cod Oriental accent.

'Are you some kind of wise guy?' I mutter.

'The compliment is accepted,' says Tzu, and he bows low.

'Is this Kieran again?' I ask Ishmael, but he stays quiet.

A microphone gets shoved too close to my face.

'Is there any meaning to your existence?' asks the old man.

'It's a lot more relevant than yours, old timer,' I tell him. 'Now get that thing out of my face before I start getting nasty.'

'Wrong answer!' booms Sun Tzu. And before I can do anything he pulls out a piece and plugs a hole in the Tommy's head. It's not pretty.

'Think very carefully about the next words you say,' whispers the old man. 'Now, why did Preston put you on the case?'

'Because I'm cheap.'

Sun Tzu aims for Ishmael but doesn't fire.

'Well, technically you're right,' says the old man, and a sheet at the back of the stage falls, revealing a Ferrari. 'And how much would it take for you to call an end to your case?'

'More money than you've got, gramps.' Which is also true. I can tell the old man's getting frustrated because he's looking for a lie. And if he wants one from me he can sing for it.

'It's good to see Ishmael back here again,' says the old man, walking over to him. Canned applause rings in my ears. 'You didn't bring so much fresh meat this time.'

'They killed Dougie,' says Ishmael.

'You're welcome.' The old man claps an arm around Ishmael's shoulders. 'Now, here's your starter for ten. What did you do with the girl?'

'The girl's with me,' I say. The old man spins and nails me with a look. 'And I've got just the ticket you've been looking for.'

The old man walks close and bends down.

'Tell me everything.'

That's when I take him out.

My fist crashes against his jaw and he's falling quicker than the Roman Empire. Sun Tzu aims the gun at me and I grab the microphone and throw it as hard as I can. When it hits Tzu in the balls you can hear the thud from the back of the room, but he goes down smiling anyway. A true professional.

'Let's go!' I snap at Ishmael, and we're up and running. But too late. The old man picks up the rocket launcher and hits me hard, and that's when the lights go out.

EIGHTEEN

When I come to I'm strapped to a chair in a basement. The old man stands before me nursing a bruise and a cup of tea. Behind him stretches an infinity of pipework and dripping faucets. It's like something out of the industrial version of Dante.

'You shouldn't have been so hasty, Mr Fury.'

'How do you know my name?' It takes all my effort to gasp that out.

'We know a lot about you, Fury. Joe Fury. We took the liberty of doing some background research while you were ... occupied.' I look in his eyes and know he's telling the truth.

'What about the dame?' I ask. 'What's her part in this scheme?'

'There's no scheme.' The old man wanders over. 'Cup of rosy?'

'Just spill the beans, gramps.' I'm in no mood for civility. 'Who's Kieran and why does Preston want him?'

'Oh dear,' says the old man with genuine regret. 'You really have been played for a fool.' He shrugs. 'Not to worry. You haven't got long for this world.'

I never figured I'd go out like this. 'Give me a smoke.'

'I'm afraid I don't approve of smoking,' says the old man. 'In fact, there's a lot I don't approve of. But somehow I'm compelled to be a part of it.'

'Cut me loose and we'll call it quits,' I offer, but he's not bargaining.

'Kieran would have my testicles for castanets,' he smiles. 'But luckily he leaves me to my hobbies.'

The old man sets the tea down on a sideboard and takes off his shirt. And suddenly I don't like where this is going.

'It's a hard life living out here.' The old man turns to face me. 'Very lonely. Very isolated. Sometimes you crave human company. Somebody to talk to, pass the time, share a nice cup of tea and a chocolate digestive with. And then ... well, then you start to get the urges.' He walks towards me. 'Strong urges. Urges that just ... overwhelm you. And that's when things get messy.' Thick steel spikes burst out of his back. He snaps his fingers and more steel spikes spring out, bursting through his skin. It's like looking at a human porcupine.

'I get your point,' I mutter lamely.

'I'll have to strip your skin for my own.' The old man creeps closer. 'I'll have to pluck your eyeballs and peel off your muscles and strip your tendons down to the bone to keep myself running.'

'Nice outfit, gramps, but I still need my smokes.'

The old man pauses. The confusion in his eyes tells me this isn't going the way he anticipated.

'I'll cut you a deal. You give me the info I want on this Kieran mug and I'll get you off his books.'

The old man hesitates. Then: 'This isn't what I want to be. I didn't want this. I wanted to be something unique.'

'You can be an opera singer for all I care—just tell me what I want to know. Kieran may think he's a tough guy, but I've seen plenty of chancers in my time. Now, you gonna keep me sitting here chewing the fat all day or you gonna let me go?'

'If you can help.'

'Just say the word.'

The old man breaks pretty easy. He must have been living in this hell for a long time and done a lot of damage to his mind to crack so easily. He levels me with an even, pleading stare, and then it all comes out.

'He lives at the end of the road. The one you started out on.'

'By the diner?'

'The very same. Just keep on down that track and you'll find him. But don't underestimate him, Mr Fury. He's a tough customer. One of the most ... complicated men I've ever had the misfortune to meet. Be wary of him. He could destroy you.'

'The only thing that could destroy me is a dame with a decent right hook.' I nod to the rope that's holding me tight. 'Now cut me loose.'

The old man drops like a stone.

NINETEEN

Ishmael stands behind him with a stupid grin on his face and a fire extinguisher in his hands. 'Thanks, Einstein,' I mutter. 'The old man was on our side.'

'But ... but ...' He looks confused. I nod to the ropes and he flicks out a switchblade and suddenly they're off.

I snap the fire to a good cigar and prod the body of the old man with my foot. The spikes have retracted and he groans, which means we won't have to dig him a goodnight bed.

'He's on our side, Ahab,' I tell Ishmael. 'The old man spilled the beans about Kieran. He's in the know and we need him. Now pick him up and let's take him with us.'

'But—'

'But nothing, smart guy.' I turn away and peer into the labyrinth of hissing pipes stretching off into the dank, dark distance. 'You slugged him, you carry him.' I jab a finger at the labyrinth. 'How far to the exit?'

It doesn't take us long. By the end of it Ishmael's sweating like a politician in a whorehouse and I'm down to the stub of my cigar. In front of us is a door in the floor.

'I should have suspected this,' I say.

Ishmael opens up the door. Nothing but blackness inside.

'Say goodnight to the kids, Gracie,' I mutter, and leap in.

TWENTY

Norman Mailer sits on a comfy chair in front of me, smoking a pipe and muttering to himself. All around us psychedelic colours spin and swirl, a miasma of visual insanity that's somehow disturbing and comforting at the same time. Sitar music plays softly in the background. Both Ishmael and the old man are gone. It's just me and Mailer.

'Goddamn woman burnt the toast again,' he mutters, jabbing the pipe at me. 'Listen, boy, and listen well. You're approaching this case all wrong. You need to think with your fists and not your head. Use the God-given talents you have for kicking the living shade out of these chumps and not thinking your way out of a situation. You understand me, boy?'

'I understand you're smoking like an old woman,' I say, snapping out a cigar and lighting it. 'This is out of your league, Mailer. You're washed up. In fact, you're not even alive.'

'Not out there,' he barks, jabbing the pipe towards the psychedelic swirl. He taps his head. 'But in here, I'm everywhere, and now I'm offering you good advice. Sound advice. Advice which may help you out one day.'

'Only if it's a one way ticket to Kieran's place.' I puff

cigar smoke at him. 'Now either cut to the chase and give me something I can use or get out of my head.'

'I'm not in your head, boy,' he laughs. 'You're in mine.'

By this point I'm up and walking. I don't move from the spot but Mailer recedes into the distance anyway. As time passes he disappears, cackling to himself, and I come up to a standard lamp sitting in the middle of nowhere. The bulb is out.

I know I shouldn't, but I snap it on anyway.

TWENTY ONE

And I'm back at the side of the road covered in dust and sand and coughing grit out of my lungs.

Ishmael sits nearby, nursing a bruised jaw. The old man stands by him, porcupined out and looking mean as hell, with his eyes fiery red.

'Kids, play nicely,' I manage to growl before pulling myself to my feet.

'Man, I love those colours during the jump,' says Ishmael, walking over to the side of the road and picking up a rock. 'What did you see, Joe?'

'Norman Mailer tried to give me advice,' I tell him. 'I think he was stoned.'

'The old Mailer route.' Ishmael nods, walking over to the old man. 'There's probably a deep message in there some-where, but I'm damned if I can figure it out.'

'Where's the car?' I look around. Nothing but the long road stretching into infinity—on one side the empty desert and on the other a huge mountain of rock.

Then a tear in the desert opens up and the shark comes barrelling out at top speed, Suzanne behind the wheel. I just have time to leap and roll, swinging up the cannon, before she slews the car to a stop, kicking up dust.

'Anyone need a ride?' she asks.

I glance at the tear, catching a glimpse of the city street with the bar and some lonely dame looking out of the window, half her face in shadow, waving me a long goodbye; and then it closes.

'Damn,' I mutter. 'Could have been a killer case.'

'The temptation didn't work, Joe,' says Suzanne. 'It would have been nothing but a shallow fabric anyway.' She holds up a bottle of bourbon. 'But we've got the car and the whisky. You want to finish this case?'

'We've got some passengers,' I tell her, and turn just as Ishmael smacks the old guy over the back of the head and knocks him flat.

'Never heard of "Help the Aged", Ahab?' I ask him, and before anyone can react Ishmael's got a knife out. He stabs into the old man's skin, tearing a huge rip down his back.

I whip out the popgun as Ishmael plunges his hands deep into the old man's back and heaves. A body comes out, covered in blood and grue—dead to everyone but Ishmael. Dougie.

The old man's skin heals up quick and fast and he gets to his feet.

'Very impressive.' I walk to the car and snap open the bottle, hitting a shot back. 'Care to tell me how?'

'How doesn't matter,' says Ishmael. 'At least he's back.'

'Used me as a bloody carrier pigeon!' The old man's not happy, and his porcupine spikes flex.

'I hate to break up the party, but I've got a job to do.' I holster the piece and climb behind the wheel of the car. 'Those who're coming get in, but don't expect any special treatment.'

Ishmael drags Dougie in, the old man seconds behind them.

'How did you find me, toots?' I ask Sue.

'Easy,' she smiles. 'Just followed the stench of self importance.'

'Pity the nuns missed,' I mutter under my breath as I reach for the key.

Ishmael lays a hand on my shoulder. 'Listen.'

Distant thunder. Deep, booming sounds. The ground vibrates. The bourbon shakes on the dashboard. Sue snaps me a worried frown and looks around. Rocks are tumbling from the mountain. Everything starts to shake big time.

I don't like this at all. I kick the car into gear and stomp on the gas. The shark peels off, leaving black streaks on the tarmac. A second later a huge mechanical foot—the size of the car—crashes down in front of us.

I slam on the brakes and we slide to a halt. Rearing up before us is a huge robot, at least a hundred feet high.

Ishmael looks like he's about to give birth, but the old man's got a smile on his face.

'Father,' he whispers.

TWENTY TWO

We're sitting in the middle of a lab on the top floor of a towering architectural nightmare. The lab is nothing but a steel ball on the top of a jagged steel stem with a staircase inside. Mathematically the place should fall right over, but the old man's father is a genius. His robot sits outside, silent.

The old man's father looks thirty. At a push. He's wearing a lab coat and the sort of expression that makes any sane man worried.

'It was Kieran who gave me the knowledge to do what I do,' he tells us, sipping a rum and coke. He's generous with the liquor, which puts him in my good books. 'Before I met him I was just a wandering scientist. I'd mix a few chemicals for the locals, knock off a few impossible fireworks—the usual. But then I met Kieran. He gave me the understanding to push myself. He would be a God, but a God would tremble at his might.'

'Is he kind to animals too?' The old man's father shoots me a withering look which has no effect. He holds out his hand.

'Call me Teffle,' he says, and then nods to the old man. 'How did you find my son?'

'The hard way.' I take a sip of the whisky. It's good.

'That was also Kieran's idea,' Teffle continues. 'A place for everyone. Inside every man there is the capacity for infinite evil and infinite justice. Well, actually that's not true, but it's the sort of thing people expect me to say. I don't know why I bother, really.'

'Father,' warns the old man.

Teffle catches himself and nods. 'Babs is right.' He smiles at the old man. Everyone else spares him a glance.

'It's short for Barbarossa,' says Babs, but nobody's convinced.

'If Kieran's the height of all wisdom, knowledge, human understanding and all that crap, why the hell does Preston want him iced?' I need answers.

'Preston works for the agency, and the agency doesn't like the competition.' Teffle's back on a roll. 'Preston and Kieran worked as a team in the old days, but Kieran's knowledge outweighed everyone he came across. Preston was a small man with a smaller mind, whose allusions only stretched to a geopolitical takeover. Kieran's ideology was much more dangerous. His ideology had a purpose before mere global politics. He believed in the beauty of chaos. And I'm afraid to say I helped him build his compound.'

'Why don't they just nuke him?' Ishmael finds his voice.

'Kieran would knock the missiles from the skies and turn them into pixie dust. Or more likely cocaine. He likes the odd snort.'

'Sounds like a goddamn wizard,' I say. 'Is there any way into his compound? Somewhere easy. Somewhere he wouldn't watch?'

'Simple,' smiles Teffle. 'Just walk through the main door.' He toasts me with the rum and then knocks it back.

I haul out the cannon and check the shells. Locked and loaded.

'Okay, Einstein, we need to get there quick and fast. Any machines in your Pandora that can help us?'

'I thought you'd never ask,' he says. The door bursts open and the nuns scream in, blazing fury.

TWENTY THREE

I'm on the floor and rolling behind the furniture as the bullets tear the place up. Babs gets up, spikes out, and swipes for one of the seven nuns, who are all bearing ugly looking machine guns. Too late. Bullets stitch up his torso and take off his head.

Teffle freezes, eyes bulging with disbelief. Suzanne races for him, firing with one hand, but she's a second too late and the bullets punch him back against a control panel, which sparks and buzzes.

Ishmael tasers Dougie who springs into life as his brother flops down dead. He jumps up into a martial arts stance I can only guess at and goes hell for fury at the nearest nun. Limbs pop and break and she's on the floor, a broken rag doll, neck and limbs twisted at impossible angles.

I'm blazing away from behind the nearest chair. Suzanne slides up close to me. 'Exit!' she yells, but there isn't one. Just a phalanx of blazing penguins and a few dead men.

Dougie goes for a second nun, but she rakes his legs with her M16 and he twists and stumbles as his kneecaps explode and he's out and down, screaming.

They don't give him or Ishmael time to sort themselves out. Four of them crowd around the brothers and pump round after round into their heads and bodies, literally turning them into twisted mush. It's not pleasant.

Suzanne sparks off a flare of Uzi fire as I let the cannon talk, and the nearest nun is cut in half and goes down. The others scatter for cover and tumble out of view: nothing in sight but the top of the odd wimple behind a piece of machinery.

A nun pops up and Suzanne lets the Uzi speak, stitching a line of holes across the floor. Then the bolt jams back as it runs out of ammo.

'Drop 'em,' shouts the nun.

I nod to Suzanne and take a puff on my cigar. She throws the Uzi across the floor and the nun tentatively peeks over the barrier she's hiding behind.

'No funny business,' the nun mutters, then comes out machine gun first and takes a step towards us. I draw on the cigar, pop the cannon over the chair and put a perfect round hole in the middle of her head. She's down and out.

The back of the room opens up with blazing gunfire and Suzanne ducks low. I don't. I've been here before.

'Smoke?' I offer Suzanne the pack of Havanas and she takes one, lighting up as the gunfire dies to a few isolated shots.

'Give up now and we won't harm you,' someone shouts.

'I've got all night, sister,' I yell. Something tells me these nuns have more than one dirty habit. You'd trust them like you'd trust a cop.

'We have orders to take you alive,' a nun shouts, and jumps up to spray a few bullets at us. 'This is just a warning.'

'Maybe you should have negotiated first,' I yell, and one of the nuns laughs. She's shushed into silence.

'Okay, funny man,' yells the negotiating nun. 'Last chance.'

'I don't die easy, sugar,' and I reach for more bullets. Except I'm empty. One left in the chamber.

'Kieran wants to talk!' yells the negotiating nun.

'I only work under my conditions, toots.' And then a familiar voice perks up from behind the nuns.

'Joe, behave.' It's Preston, and he's standing as tall as day behind the nuns, still wearing his waitress uniform. I guess he likes it.

TWENTY FOUR

'I don't get it, Preston,' I yell. 'Why the nuns? You always told me you were an atheist.'

'We all meet strange bedfellows, Joe,' he shouts back. 'Now come with me and we'll make our peace together.'

'Nice offer but I don't swing that way, Preston. Now tell the penguins to back off or we're all in for a long night.'

'This isn't a deal situation, Joe.' Smugly Preston hefts an M16 with a grenade launcher under the barrel. 'It's shit or quit.'

'Why do you need me to get to Kieran? You were practically brothers.'

'An introduction, Joe.' Preston wanders over to a piece of bullet-peppered machinery and starts caressing the twisted wires and ruptured metal. 'We fell out of trust and you were the only person who could bring him back. I need you, Joe.'

'I don't get it. Just go with the nuns. They'll take you straight to him.'

'For a smart detective you certainly have a slow mind,' says Preston. 'They don't know Kieran. They can't take me to him. They're here for the girl.'

'What's she done?'

'You don't want to know,' says Preston. I look at Suzanne and she looks back, and there's guilt in her eyes. Deep guilt. Whatever she's done, it's not pretty.

'Let the girl go and we can talk.' I make sure the single bullet is in the chamber and ready myself.

'We need you, Joe,' says Preston, and I'm up on my feet with the gun to my head and my arm round the girl's neck.

'One shot and I'm history,' I tell him. He smiles patronisingly, then whips up the M16 and shoots before I can do anything. The bullet takes Suzanne dead centre of the heart and knocks her down. She's gone before she hits the floor. I swing the gun round and blast off the shot, but Preston's already moved. He chokes a laugh, but I made the heel sweat.

'Now let's negotiate like real men,' says Preston, gesturing to a chair. I chew the stem of the cheroot and feel in my pocket. The watch the monk gave me.

I look down at the body. I've no idea if this is right or wrong, if this is the time to use it, but I don't have a choice. It's either hell or high water.

'Adios, creep,' I growl, and press the button on the top of the watch.

It's Hell.

TWENTY FIVE

Literally Hell. Fire, brimstone—the lot. A jagged landscape of the hellspawn stretching out into infinity in every direction— towering fireballs reaching to the endless, black sky.

I'm on a road that curves off in either direction. And there's no sign of Suzanne. Bad news. I glance at the watch. It's stopped. I click it again, it starts ticking, and for a second I'm back in the lab with the bodies and the nuns and Preston looking confused.

'Wait,' he shouts, but I click the button again and I'm back in Hell.

A black carriage made of bone, lead by two screaming banshees, approaches, the demonic, horned figure at the reins urging the skeletal horses onwards. The demon pulls up. All horns and jagged, stone teeth.

'*Shut up!*' it screams at the banshees, and they fall silent.

'Long time, Chronos,' I say, sparking up a stoogie from the flaming fingertip the demon offers. 'How's it hanging?'

Chronos points to a jagged tree in the distance, writhing with the souls of suicide victims. He lets out a throaty chuckle. 'To what do I owe this pleasure, Joe?' The voice sounds like broken glass.

'Looking for a corpse. Suzanne something, killed a few minutes ago. I need a favour.'

'What are you willing to bargain with, Joe?' hisses Chronos, leering down.

'Me not kicking your ragged ass all over this place,' I tell him. And he knows I mean it.

'Not my jurisdiction,' he says, straightening up. 'Try a man called Chicago who lives in Despair, first city of Hell.'

'You taking me there?'

'Only if you're a corpse.' And with that he's off, banshees wailing away, disappearing into the fire. I puff my cigar and take a look at the citadel in the distance, all black steel and blood. It's going to be a long walk.

TWENTY SIX

The problem with Hell is the environment. It's always uphill. You try turning downhill and you're walking uphill again. It's not painful—it's just a drag. Something you can do without.

The first place I come across is a fast food joint. Weathered, empty grey faces peer out from the inside. Anyone behind the counter has already had their soul sucked out of them by the time they get there. When they pay their penance this is where they end up. But I am hungry for information.

I walk in and look for the freshest body. A truck driver with a huge shard of glass bisecting his head.

'You compos mentis?' I ask the corpse, and he looks at me, confused for a moment, then nods.

'Who's running the show around here now?' I ask him.

'Well, ever since they privatised it things have gone downhill.' He picks at the grey slab of meat in front of him. The meat turns around and blinks a single eyeball at him, before crawling off the table and making a break for it. 'It's not the place it used to be.'

'You look fresh. How do you know?'

'I hear things,' the body mutters. 'Want to hear some music?' And he grabs the shard of glass and starts sawing it back and forth, the glass grating on bone. Obviously a fortnight short of a week.

'Anyone else in here got a mind of their own?' I yell, looking around.

'I have.' A single voice pops up. Some guy in a raincoat and trilby smoking a cigarette in the shadows in the far corner. I walk over.

'You're a long way from home,' I tell him, and he nods.

'Pull up a cloud, wiseguy, we've got business.'

I take a seat.

'The man you're looking for is Steps Mackenzie. He's taken over this joint pretty quick, see, and he's gunning to franchise it out. Hell's not bringing the Mickeys in and Steps is a greedy man. You see what I'm saying?'

'He's aiming to take over topside.'

'You're not just a pretty face, wiseguy.' The figure snaps his brim. 'You want a ride, just call out for Mugsy. Tell him I sent you.' He creases a half smile and then seems to disappear into the shadows.

I leave the joint with the shard man still playing his head like a fiddle. Outside it's chaos and madness.

'Mugsy!'

A finger taps me on the back. I turn, and if this is Mugsy then he's not happy to see me. Mainly since I plugged him ten years ago after he escaped from the big house. It paid for my car.

'Finally made it down here, then?' Mugsy smiles a very sick smile. I should land him a solid right, but something tells me I might need him.

'I'm only visiting. I'm looking for someone.'

'Good luck. There's a million lost souls down here.'

'You know I don't believe any of that crap, Mugsy,' I say, and blow smoke in his face. 'Someone told me to call for you, and I have, and you're here, and for some reason he thinks you can help me. You gonna help, or do I put you down a second time?'

Mugsy chews this over. Then nods.

'You're not gonna like what you see.'

TWENTY SEVEN

The processing factory. Steam vents and huge funnels and churning machinery. The place looks like a giant slaughterhouse with everything five times bigger than it's meant to be.

A row of people shunt along a rack, upside down with meathooks through their ankles.

'Okay, here's where we process 'em,' says Mugsy, pointing

to the bodies. He nods to a yawning furnace at the end of the rack. 'Right in the centre of the first city of Hell. They go through there, all consuming fire, baddabing—come out the other side ready for the proper show. We got an entire valley full of processors just to assign punishments. Is that progress or what? You remember the old days when the horned assholes used to poke people with pitchforks. Man, I love the reformation. Screwed this place up good.'

'You're all heart, Mugsy,' I tell him. 'I'm looking for—'

'I know, I know,' he interrupts, waving me quiet. 'I knew when she turned up. Had the stench about her. Goddamn do-gooders. Come on.'

Mugsy leads the way out of the processing hall and into a quiet office. You can still hear the screams, but it's less of a distraction.

'Take a seat.' Mugsy nods to a chair. 'I got someone who wants to talk to you.'

He leaves and the figure from the fast food joint enters. For some reason, no matter where he goes, half his face is always in shadow.

'You made it,' he says.

'You could have brought me here yourself!'

He smiles at that and nods. 'Don't like to carry my own dirty washing.'

The figure takes a seat. 'You can call me Chicago. Suzanne's fine and ready. Plucky dame.'

'She's got more moxy than most of the skirt I know.'

He chuckles. 'You'll get her back regardless, but right now I need a favour off you. A big one. One that guarantees you a one way ticket out of here.'

'I prefer to make my own rules, Chicago, but I'm willing to listen.' I settle back for the big reveal.

'Take out Steps for me.' Chicago leans forward, serious. 'I'd do it myself, but my face is too well known around these parts. He's got ties with Kieran.'

'That joker gets everywhere,' I say.

'Kieran's got a lot of fingers in a lot of pies.'

'Okay,' I say, nodding. 'What happens if I do take him out? What then?'

'You get the girl and get back to topside.'

I finger the watch in my pocket and Chicago flicks his eyes to it. He knows.

'You can forget about that trinket. It doesn't work anymore.'

I pull it out and press the button. He's right.

'Take out Steps and you're back on the road.'

'Why me?' I ask.

'Because you're the only one I can rely on.' He leans back, a hint of a smile on his face. 'Besides, I thought you might like the challenge.'

'I'll need the girl first.'

Chicago shakes his head. 'She stays here.'

'No dice, Chicago. Give me the broad or the deal's off.'

He studies me. Then nods.

'You know, if I don't, I get the feeling I might regret it.' He leans back and yells over his shoulder. 'Bring her in!'

Mugsy leads Sue into the office. He's nursing a bruised jaw, so I figure she didn't come easy.

'You took your time,' she says.

'Consider it done,' I tell Chicago, and then the ceiling explodes.

TWENTY EIGHT

A giant steel claw slams down into the room and grabs Mugsy round the waist, wrenching tight and slicing him cleanly in two.

'Get out of here!' yells Chicago. He pulls out a popgun and starts blazing away at the steel claw as it gropes around for another victim.

I don't need telling twice. I grab Sue and we're out of the door quick, straight into a world of chaos.

Demons and muties and creatures are spilling through the factory, some with guns and some with blades. A hulking green creature with multi-horned head, a fistful of eyeballs and a jutting jaw spins an ugly looking cannon at me and I slam my elbow into its face, sending it down and out.

Sue picks up the cannon and starts blasting a path through the chaos. A ninja wielding a wakizashi sword comes at me and I spin and straight arm him and he goes down for the count. I stamp on his face to make sure he's learnt his lesson and then we're off again.

Something with heads where its hands should be comes at us, snapping away. Sue gets caught on the arm and almost drops the cannon, but I grab the two snapping heads and slam them together. Sue kicks it in the crotch for good measure, then turns the gun on a phalanx of ravenous, red-eyed Leprechauns who are spilling through the main door.

'Let's make an exit.' Sue turns the gun on the wall and starts firing shell after shell into it. The steel warps, buckles and then explodes outwards and suddenly we're out in the fires of Hell.

It's worse outside. Something big and ugly with jagged steel spikes on its legs is tearing down the city's main street. Buildings crash in its wake and tortured souls shriek fresh peals of pain. This is something they didn't bargain for when it came to eternal damnation. All I can see above the legs are too many teeth and too many eyes.

'Where's my mommy!'

The voice is like nails down a blackboard. We turn and there's a small girl with rosy cheeks and a flowery dress holding a lollipop and a balloon. Sue levels the cannon at the creature as it smiles a gap-toothed smile, blowing it into history and leaving nothing in its place but a lot of smoke and a pair of hands holding an egg whisk and a cheese grater. It could have been nasty.

'Good call,' I tell her, and we start beating a hasty retreat down a street littered with twisted bodies.

I glance behind me. Whatever the thing with the teeth, eyes and spiked legs is, it's zeroed in on us and is starting to catch up.

'Time for a miracle,' I mutter, and a solid rope falls down in front of us, keeping pace.

TWENTY NINE

'Hang on!' I catch Sue around the waist and grab for the rope and look up. Above us is a helicopter and, just visible, Chicago at the controls.

The helicopter rises, taking us up, and the eyes and teeth

creature starts to double its pace, pealing out an ear shattering roar. Sue spins in my arms, turns the cannon on the thing and starts blasting away at it.

Eyes explode and teeth shatter but the thing keeps coming. A huge boiling arm of fire comes reaching up for us. The rope jerks sideways and I look ahead and there's a glass building blocking the way.

'Brace yourself,' I warn, and hold Sue tight. We crash through the glass, shards spinning, and land on our feet as the rope slips away. We start running, tearing through the office building as the blazing arm smashes into the glass wall and sends fire roaring out behind us.

Straight ahead I can see the only way out. Right through the glass and fourteen storeys straight down. But I keep on running because there's no escape behind us.

We both take a leap and smash through the glass just as the rope hovers into view. I reach, grab, snap an arm around Sue and suddenly we're off again, sailing high over the blazing buildings, leaving the cavernous roar of the eyes and teeth creature behind us.

'You got any shells left in that cannon?' I nod to the oversized popgun and Sue checks the breach and nods. 'A few. Why?'

'We've got company.' Huge, mutant helicopters spin around the building we just vacated, part machine and part demon, their front ends wide open mouths and blood red eyes. Clawed feet are hunched up in the underbellies, while the rotors buzz out of the creatures' backs. They carry big, ugly guns fifty feet long, and they don't look friendly.

'Time for a smoke,' I mutter, and Sue spins the cannon on the 'copters and starts raking them with shells, knocking chunks out of the skin and blasting the rotors into shattered bone shards.

But this is just a distraction. I turn in time to see something bigger and meaner than anything I've ever seen.

'Damn, I thought he was long gone,' I manage, before a huge frosty claw plucks us out of the sky. We're pulled up and up until we're looking straight at an impossibly wide face.

'Hello, Joe,' booms the creature. 'Long time no see.'

'Sue, meet Bob, the ruler of Hell.'

THIRTY

It's cold on the hand of the ruler of Hell. Sue huddles up and Chicago sits pensively by as we stride through the burning wasteland towards the towering citadel in the distance, where Steps Mackenzie rules.

'You losing your touch or something?' I yell at Bob. 'Remember when all this used to be ice? What the hell happened to it?'

'You can't hold back progress.' Bob sighs. 'Besides, Steps offered me an easy retirement and I took the opportunity.'

'Who the hell is this asshole?' I ask.

'I don't know,' says Bob, shrugging his shoulders. Ice splinters and cracks on his skin. 'He's just ... convincing.'

'He's obviously convinced you to turn into a heel,' I yell, and despite myself I'm angry. 'Grow some balls.'

'I can't,' booms Bob. 'He took them off me. He convinced me to hand them over and ... well ... that's what happened.'

'Jesus, Bob!' I shout, and turn away in disgust. It's a bad day in Hell when the ruler gets hoodwinked into handing over his cojones.

I sit down next to Chicago and spark up a cigar.

'Got any ideas how to get out of this one, wise guy?' I ask him, and he shakes his head and stares off into the eternal flames.

'I think we just lost the initiative.' He puffs out a peel of smoke and then throws the butt of his cigarette over the side of Bob's hand. It spirals down and a jagged-beaked human vulture swoops and snatches it out of the air.

'Or maybe not.' I have an idea.

THIRTY ONE

It doesn't take long for Bob to hand us over to the guards. I consider taking a few out, but Chicago just shakes his head and silently warns me off. Something tells me he has a trick up his sleeve.

They tie our hands behind our backs, take away our cannons and lead us away.

The stately throne room of Steps Mackenzie is the living

embodiment of over-indulgence. If a surface isn't plated in gold it's studded with diamonds. The throne itself is made of human skulls, all of them with gags in their mouths to stop them complaining.

Steps himself is a small guy, but too many steroids have pumped his body up and left his head looking like a peanut on an oversized torso.

Chicago is his first port of call.

'Ya weasel,' he spits. Chicago doesn't budge. 'Ya thought you could take me out? Ya thought you could get the drop on me, huh? Ya thought you could take on Steps Mackenzie and get away with it? Well, I guess I showed you, ya goddamn low life no good nobody.'

'You talk big for such a small man.' The mocking smile on Chicago's face makes it all the worse.

'I'm gonna take ya down, Chicago, ya hear me!' rages Steps. 'I'm gonna take ya right down and bury you so goddamn deep you'll never get back to the top, do ya hear me?'

'I don't hear nothing, Steps.' Chicago is cool as a cucumber. 'All I can see is your jaw flapping and nothing coming out. I bet you don't even have the moxy to take on my pal here.' He turns to me and nods. 'Isn't that right, Joe?'

I'm quick to catch on. 'Pint size like him. I bet his mother still puts him to bed.'

Steps is over like a shot. 'You leave my mother out of this!' His finger is right up to my face, but I shoot him a look that says I know he still wets the bed. He shakes and shivers with rage and then slaps me hard and fast around the jaw.

I take it, and then straighten up. 'That's gonna cost you, Steps. You're just a cheap punk who's got a big mouth, and you know you're going down. Touch me again and it's bedtime for Bonzo.'

This throws him into a spin. You can tell by the look in his eyes that he's torn between kicking my teeth into next Tuesday and slapping Chicago down until he says 'uncle.' Luckily I resolve the dispute for him.

'Hey, Steps,' I yell. He spins around. 'Here's how to sing soprano.' And I lay the mother of all kicks into his balls.

That does the trick. He goes down for the count. A man that small had no right to be wearing Bob's balls, and once the pain starts spreading through him he starts to understand what having a real set actually means.

'Mama!' he croaks, and then he keels over and starts moaning like a wounded dog.

'Untie us,' Chicago snaps at the guards, and they swap glances, uncertain.

'Untie them!' booms the voice of Bob, shattering glass, and before we know it we're free. I rub the pain out of my wrists as Chicago sits down on the throne.

'Nice touch, Joe,' he says. 'You got the moves where it counts.'

'We free to go?' I ask him, and he nods. I grab Sue by the hand and take out the pocket watch. 'In which case, I'll see you on the flipside.'

'That won't work again,' Chicago tells me. 'You had two pops and that's the end of it. I'll take you the old fashioned way.' And he snaps his fingers.

A second later we're back in Teffle's improbable lab. Preston and the nuns are gone, but in their place is a giant chicken with a gun. 'Welcome to the brotherhood,' says the chicken. 'Would you like to make a donation?'

THIRTY TWO

We're all in the giant robot, stamping our way down the dark and dusty road. Night has fallen, the shark is nestled safely in the robot's claw, and the giant chicken is at the controls.

'The League of Crime Fighting Chickens! That's what he wanted to call us.' The chicken shakes his head and sighs. 'It was all a big joke. "Yeah, let's make fun of the chickens—what can they do to harm us?" Well, these suckers will soon find out.'

'You're the first talking chicken I ever met,' I say. 'How did this happen?'

'You can probably guess if you think hard enough,' the chicken replies, and then turns his weary head to the road.

'Kieran,' says Sue, and swaps me a glance. 'I heard about this back in yonder. Teffle was against the experiment because it served no purpose. Giant sentient chickens were an evolutionary anomaly, but Kieran went ahead and did it anyway.'

'The man's a sadist,' says the chicken. 'I didn't even know if I was happy or unhappy pecking grain on the farm, but I know I'm not happy now. And neither are the rest of us.'

'How many of you are there?' I ask.

'Enough.' The chicken glowers, and there's something unhealthy in his look. 'He wanted a crime fighting league so he brought in a martial arts expert to teach us everything we know. Pushed us to limits neither man nor beast has ever been pushed to before, and all the while in our hearts the seeds of revolution were growing. You don't cross a chicken with a grudge and expect to get away with it. Eventually that man is going to rue the day he ever genetically mutated a phalanx of giant chickens and taught them martial arts.'

The chicken takes his wings off the controls and starts flashing through a series of killer moves, which would be impressive if I wasn't concentrating on smoking my cheroot. He returns to the controls and guides the robot down the road with a steely determination.

'Chicken-fu,' he mutters. 'The most deadly martial art known to humanity. Dangerous in its unpredictability.' In the distance we see the glow of lights. The chicken points a wing. 'Base camp.'

As we approach I can see the chickens lined up in rows, drilling themselves through the motions, wing and claw cutting through the air with killer accuracy. Any man could see these chickens have been training hard for revenge.

'But where's my manners?' tuts the chicken. 'I haven't even introduced myself. My name is Justice, and I cordially invite you to dinner.'

THIRTY THREE

Of course, it was chicken feed.

THIRTY FOUR

We sit around the table, surrounded by surly-faced giant talking ninja chickens. These look like the kind of chickens who grew up on the wrong side of the tracks. They've seen the dark side of life and want revenge.

Justice pours a round of clarets for everyone and then raises his glass in a toast.

'To the end of Kieran.' He knocks back the claret and everyone joins in. Justice slams the glass down.

'For too long we have lived under this man's tyranny,' he begins. 'For too long we have suffered under the chains he binds us with. We are used and abused as his playthings and projects and when we've fulfilled our brief we're cast aside into the desert to fend for ourselves. But, I say, "no longer." No longer should we have to be subject to his twisted schemes, for we are chickens, and we shall rise up against our oppressors, and we shall cast him out of the temple he has built for himself and lead our brothers into a new dawn of peace and plenty!'

The chickens around the table roar with pride and raise their glasses for another toast. Glasses clink, chickens cluck, but I lean back and spark a stoogie and wait for the self congratulation to take a holiday.

'Pretty words, Justice,' I say. 'But there's a big distance between words and deeds. How do you plan to stick it to the man? With this?' I cast a plateful of chicken feed across the table.

'No, my friend.' Justice leans forward and points a wing at me. 'With you.'

'What gives you the big idea I'd help a down-on-his-luck chicken with a grudge?'

'Because I see the fire in your eyes,' says Justice, leaning towards me. 'I see the passion within you to do the right thing. I see the revolutionary zeal in your spirit, and it fills my heart with burning pride.'

'I see a lot of hot air.' I blow a puff of smoke in his face and he coughs and sits back.

Justice contemplates for a second. 'Okay, see it like this. When you bust through the main doors we can be there as a distraction. The more heat we take off you the easier it'll be to land a hand on Kieran. We're both winners.'

'I like your style, Cogburn.' I jab the cigar at him. 'Keep a feather out for us and make sure you're there when we hit the compound. Any clues you can give us about it.'

'Just watch your ass, Mr Fury,' says Justice. 'Whatever tricks you think you've got up your sleeve, Kieran's already thought of them.' He leans forward once more. 'One more thing. Watch out for the samurai.'

THIRTY FIVE

Justice and his ninja chickens see us off with a fond farewell as we tail off in the shark, and soon we're back on the road and tearing down the strip.

'We can trust 'em,' says Sue. 'A chicken with a grudge is nothing to laugh at.'

'What's your connection to Kieran, sister?' I spare her a glance. 'And what have the nuns got to do with it?'

Sue gives me a long, studied stare and then fesses up. 'I knew him a long time ago. We were close. Then things went wrong and he couldn't stand to be rejected. So he carted me away to the Sisters of the Immaculate Immolation and that's where I've been for the last ten years.'

'So why are they after you?'

'They have a "no get out" clause. If you leave, you die.' Sue stares out at the passing scenery and sighs. 'That's why Kieran put me in there. He couldn't bring himself to kill me, and he figured I'd make a break for it the first opportunity I got, so he could live safe in the knowledge that the nuns would pop a cap in my rear loader and he wouldn't be directly responsible for me pushing up the daisies.'

'Sweet story, sister,' I grumble. 'But you're not telling me an ounce of the truth.'

She looks back. She knows I can tell she's lying. 'It's a long story,' she says.

'It's a long road.'

She looks at me hard and I know the sister's been through a rough time. But I've heard a thousand sob stories.

'It started when the earth tore in two—' she mutters, and then stops as the ground shakes.

'If it's the robot again I'm gonna plug it,' I say, whipping out the popgun and glancing behind us. But it's not coming from behind. A roar breaks through the growl of the shark's engine and suddenly a triceratops comes sliding into our path, three horns aiming right for the grille.

THIRTY SIX

I slam on the brakes and the shark screams to a halt, leaving a trail of tyre tracks in our wake. Sue pops off a few rounds with the Uzi, but they bounce off the triceratops's carapace. It shakes its head and looks pissed off, then charges right for us.

'Hang on.' I hit reverse and the shark bites the tarmac and screams back the way we came, but this prehistoric monster is fast. Too fast.

The lead horn hits the bumper and the dinosaur flips its head, and we're spinning like a bottle off the road and into the dirt. I'm up and out and Sue's already in front of me, tearing over the landscape as the thunderous roar of the creature looms up behind us.

But they're not taking me without a fight. I skid to a stop and spin, hefting the cannon up and aiming down the barrel as the beast rages towards us.

'Suck on the stone age!' I mutter, and blast off a shot that slams straight into the eye. The triceratops screeches to a bloody halt and shakes its head, and I'm starting to wonder if the Poindexters are wrong and their brains are in their ass.

'Keep it real, Joe,' screams Sue, and she lays a blast of white hot lead over the face of the massive beast. It roars and bucks and bleeds, then starts to look angry.

'Hang tight, sister.' I grab her around the waist. 'This could be a road trip we'll never forget.'

And then the ground below the beast buckles and splits, and a hand slams out from under the dinosaur and straight into its guts. A second later it yanks out the beasts entrails as another fist punches up and into the animal.

A body emerges from under the creature and heaves the thing as it wails and cries, then picks it up and topples it over onto its side. The figure stands up.

It's Sun Tzu.

THIRTY SEVEN

'Nice party trick, Tzu,' I tell the figure. 'You back for another game show or here for the sushi?'

Tzu steps forward and lends us a cordial bow. I follow, along with Sue.

'To what do we owe this pleasure?' I ask, sparking up a Havana. 'You're a little off your limits.'

'The game show was just a formality,' says Tzu. 'You must forgive me for that little sideshow. I was being spiritually held hostage by the old man, and now you have freed me.'

'Thanks, but I didn't free you.' I tap ash into the blasted eye socket of the fallen dinosaur. 'The old man died in a fire-fight. Now cough up the beans, wiseguy, or your jawbone takes a holiday it never forgets.'

'It is no coincidence that you are here,' says Tzu. 'The formalities of your existence have led you to this point in your life where you can now take part in your greatest challenge.'

'Nice speech, but I'm on a case.' I jab the stoogie at him. 'Make with the details.'

'We are here as combatants in the greatest battle of the century between man and beast,' says Tzu, looking honoured. 'We have been chosen from the finest combat artists in the world to compete in a tournament. A tournament of death.'

'The chicken was right,' I growl. 'We were warned about you.'

'The chicken?' Sun Tzu spits. 'The chicken is foul.'

'Cut the stand-up,' I tell him. 'If you get in our way we'll cut you down. Now take a hike and don't bother us again.'

'If we beat our enemies I will join you on your quest,' says Tzu. 'It would be an honour to fight beside such a legend.'

'You got your wires crossed, Mac.' I start towards the shark. 'I'm nothing but a shoestring. Have a nice life.'

But before I get anywhere near the car the ground starts to rumble again. This isn't good. I turn to Tzu and he looks pleased, which also isn't good.

There's a dust cloud in the distance, a low thunder filling the air. Sue snaps another clip into the Uzi and cocks the hammer.

'Let's get out of here.' I'm off towards the shark and she's behind me, but the dust cloud gets bigger and the thunder gets louder and suddenly we're surrounded by dinosaurs of all shapes and sizes.

THIRTY EIGHT

Sun Tzu sits astride a tyrannosaurus and waves a wakizashi sword in the air.

'Come join us, honourable one,' he yells over the roars and screams of the dinosaur army. 'It is the only way out of here.'

'Why, of all the luck,' I mutter.

An army grunt on a stegosaurus comes towards us, with the reins of a megalosaurus in one hand and an M60 in the other. The megalosaurus rears up on its hind legs, roars, and raps its sharp thumbs together. It's big, mean and ugly.

'I thought these didn't exist,' I say to the grunt as he hands me the reins. He laughs.

'Everything exists in this fight,' he says. He kicks the side of the steg and they canter off into the crowd of monsters.

'We'd better see this one through,' I tell the dame, and I'm up on the dinosaur, with her holding tight behind me. We make our way to the front of what seems to be an endless line of prehistoric creatures.

Across an empty expanse of desert we see another, equally long, line of dinosaurs.

'Any tactics?' asks Sue.

I nod. 'Keep firing and look for an exit.'

Sun Tzu rides along our line of creatures, his sword held high.

'We fight for a victory that doesn't exist!' he yells. 'We fight for a worthless piece of desert. We fight for our lives and our deaths, and we fight for the honour of battle. For anything else would be a lie, and anything else would be an excuse. We fight because we have to, and we will fight until we die. Let me make this clear, we are doing this for no reason whatsoever, and these pitiful words mean nothing at all, and in the end it's all completely worthless!'

The crowd roars.

'I wonder how many miles this thing does to the gallon,' I mutter, checking out the meg. Tzu turns to face the enemy in front of us.

'To glory!' he screams, kick starting the rex, and we're streaming off in a cloud of sweat, roars and thunderous noise towards a certain death.

THIRTY NINE

My meg gets a good lick in to something big and slimy with too many teeth. It tears a chunk out of the creature and I pop a cap in its eye and it goes down, squealing and spitting blood.

Sue turns the Uzi on another monster behind us as it rears up, with hate in its eyes and blood on its fangs. She takes out its knees, and as it stumbles forwards I haul the meg out of the way. The creature crashes to the ground and spills its rider.

I wrench the reins to the right and come face to face with a steg carrying a Viking who's toting a rocket launcher.

'Duck!' I scream as the launcher belches fire. The rocket flies right over our heads and explodes against something mean and nasty, and suddenly we're off the meg and on the floor.

Nothing but feet and screams around us. I spin and fire a few rounds off, taking out some riders, then turn to face the biggest, meanest, ugliest looking dinosaur I've ever set eyes on. And it's cased head to neck in battle armour.

The creature bends low, bares a universe of razor sharp teeth and lets out a roar right into my face. I slam my fist into its jaw and send it reeling to the floor, out cold.

'Stay!' I tell it, then haul the meg back on to its feet and suddenly we're up again and trying to find a way through this mess.

Blood flies everywhere and we spin and fire. The meg gets a few good licks in with its horned thumbs and razor teeth, and soon enough there's space around us. And beyond the space, chaos.

Sun Tzu comes riding up covered in blood with his eyes on fire. 'This is the greatest honour,' he screams, then he's off, hacking and slashing and making sure the enemy stay down.

'We've gotta get out of here,' yells Sue, and I look for an exit, but there isn't one.

'We'll have to fight our way out.' And I aim the popgun at the nearest beast and take out the rider. The creature screams and roars and, without any guidance, starts taking chunks out of everything around it.

I turn to see a diplodocus coming straight for us; and one thing's for sure, this creature wasn't a weed eater. It's got corpses in its mouth and more teeth than a gameshow host.

Sue sparks off a line of fire while I kick the meg into action. The dip swings its massive head for us and clamps down hard on the meg's haunches, bringing it down.

Sue rolls, leaps up and jams the Uzi right against the dip's skull, blasting round after round into its head, and tearing its flesh into a memory. The huge creature manages a wounded roar before keeling over and crushing flat a Pashtun warrior who's aiming an old bolt action rifle at us. Sue kicks the corpse for good luck.

'Nice shooting, toots.' I reload and look for a sign to lead us out of this insanity.

'Any suggestions?' She snaps another clip into the Uzi and chambers a round.

'Start praying,' and we both aim in the same direction and start to carve ourselves a path.

And there, through the carnage, I spot the battered wreck of the shark. It looks a mess, but it's something to aim for.

'This way.' Sue follows my lead and we start to blast a way through the prehistoric mayhem. Kneecaps explode and riders go down and we dodge and duck and weave our way through the teeth and claws and swords and guns. It's a miracle, but we make it through the melee in one piece. The car looks like last year's scrap heap.

'That's going to need some fixing up,' says Sue.

'Give me a monkey wrench and some time and we'll see what we can do.'

Then Sue gets zapped by a blue light and the next second we're on the deck of a spaceship, staring down the wrong end of a laser blaster wielded by a three-headed alien.

FORTY

I check my pockets. No matches.

'Anyone got a light?' I hold up the cigar. The laser speaks and the tip glows red. 'Thanks.' I take a puff and give the aliens the once over. Two of them. Three heads. Four arms. Skinny as rakes. 'What do you jokers want?'

'Are you the one they call "Kieran"?' says Alien No. 1.

'What's the beef?' I ask.

Alien No. 2 holds up a mangled piece of technology with

wires hanging off it, bleeping weakly. 'He sold us this dodgy piece of equipment. We want his testicles in a jar.'

'You got the wrong schmo,' I tell them. 'I'm looking for him myself. Any clues?'

Alien No. 1 clips Alien No. 2 around the back of the middle head. 'I told you he was the wrong puny earthling scum,' it says. 'Why can you never get the co-ordinates right?'

'Can't you beam down there and give him a piece of your wisdom, ET?' I saunter across and scan the flight deck of whatever I'm in. Cut price alien technology. Straight out of Roswell and not half as advanced. 'Where the hell did you jokers come from?'

'The Nebula Cortex,' says Alien No. 1. 'But our generator packed up many of your earth years ago and now we have been forced to seek out the help of you pitiful earthling creatures for our spare parts. Our ancestors mock us every Terran night from their astro-beds and we live in shame.'

'Cut the chatter,' I snap, taking control. 'Got any whisky?'

'Ah,' nods Alien No. 1. 'Shouting fluid. Yes, we have a few baubles of it. It helps power our spaceship.'

And with that Alien No. 1 pops out a bottle of cheap whisky and pours me a splash. I knock it back, slam it down, and contemplate a way out of this.

'Okay, Gort,' I say. 'You need parts, and we need out of here. I'll cut you a deal. How good are you at repairs?'

'The very best,' nods Alien No. 2.

'You fix up the shark and we'll talk about getting your generator back on line. I know a guy down the road who knows a thing or two about particle generators and alien technology.'

Alien No. 1 looks disapprovingly at me. 'You are the alien to us, earth man.'

'Shut up.'

It shuts up.

FORTY ONE

The aliens whip up a storm in their repairs bay and before you know it the shark's back up and running like it's straight off the production line. I take a few more pops of whisky and we're beamed down to the road, just outside The Shack.

It's a rickety, falling down building which looks like it was stacked together out of driftwood. I push open the door and inside it's a mess of wires and mechanical parts and bits and pieces thrown all over the place.

'Ginger!' I shout, and a head pops out from behind a stack of spare parts. Ginger gives us the once over and then walks out.

'Cor blimey, strike a light, me old china,' he mutters, and shoves out a grease stained hand to greet us. 'What's the apple and Barry.'

'We've got a problem, Ginger,' I tell him, nodding to the aliens. Ginger doesn't bat an eyelid. 'Engine repairs.'

'Right, me old squirrel and saucer,' he nods. 'Spaceship. Fifty to the tonne. Nice little speeder, I've heard.'

'Greetings, strange talking cockney.' Alien No. 1 steps forward. 'We must hurry before the Klaxons of Narg infiltrate our system.'

'Hold yer horses, me nutkin pie.' Ginger holds up a warning hand. 'We've got plenty of time for the greaser's palm. Give us a nod and scratch down Strawberry Lane and we'll see about the China's roller skates.'

'What can you offer him as a barter?' I translate for the aliens.

'We have this.' Alien No. 1 pulls out a bright shining orb which fills the dank, dusty interior of the shack. Ginger spares it a disparaging glance.

'Got fifty of them,' he says, nodding to a stack of glowing orbs at the back. 'Anyfing else?'

The aliens swap worried glances.

'What would you like, earth filth?' they ask simultaneously.

'Got a Stillson wrench?' asks Ginger. 'Me uvver one's spannered and shite, ain't it.'

'Er ... yes.' The aliens conflab for a second and then one of them stands up, presses a button on its chest and a Stillson wrench pops out of thin air.

Ginger gives it a good heft and then nods.

'Like it. Give us half an hour. Transport the scrotey old minger into me pot luck corner and we'll see about skiffling the trifle.'

'Spaceship—repair bay,' I say to the aliens.

The roof of the shack opens up and the spaceship levitates down into the work area. Huge steel clamps heave out and pull it into place.

Seconds later Ginger's up to his arms in grease, the underside of the ship open, tearing out trails of wires and muttering about the shoddy workmanship of your average alien vessel.

'The problem is, guv, you just can't get the parts these days,' he says to me. 'They're all bleedin' knock-offs, innay?'

I hunker down next to him.

'Ginger, I need some info on someone called Kieran—no last name.'

He scoots out from beneath the spaceship and fixes me with a steady gaze.

'Okay then, old boy.' All pretence of the loveable cockney rogue drops from his voice. 'The man's a dashed brute, but a phenomenal boxer. He's a cad, a swine, a swindler, a rogue and a gadabout but, by god, he's the most inspiring man I've ever had dealings with.'

'Go on.'

'He's got some sort of bally fortress at the end of the road, old chap.' Ginger wipes his hands on an oily rag and stares me square in the eye. 'I did some work for him setting up—bounder told me he was putting some sort of doomsday device together. Total hogwash, of course—just some sort of dashed portable toilet. But the funny thing is, he has this way of completely hoodwinking you into his way of thinking. What's the interest in him?'

'Preston hired me to take him in.'

'That old tranny.' Ginger chuckles. 'Bit of a queer sort. Bats on the wrong side of the pavilion, if you know what I mean.'

'Is there any way I can get in without attracting attention.'

Ginger pulls out a fork from his trouser pocket and hands it to me.

'Try this on the front door.'

'Will it get me in?'

'No, but it'll keep the bally thing jammed tight while you get in through the storm drain.' Ginger gets up and pats the spaceship. 'Don't expect to go in topside, either. I designed the defences. This little number will be blown out of the sky before you've had time to pull your socks up. Just look for the storm drain with the green tag on it. That'll take you straight to the main complex. After that you're on your own.'

'Thanks, Ginger.' I shake his hand.

'The pleasure's all mine,' he says, and then looks over my shoulder at the aliens. 'Oh well, back to the show for the tourists.'

Ginger walks around me and straight over to the aliens.

'Luvva duck, me old cockney sparra cor blimey strikes a lights,' he says, slapping each of them on the shoulder. 'Fixed up like a kipper before the lampshade has time to make a biscuit.'

'All ready to go,' I translate. The aliens nod.

'Well done, earth scum. Now we are ready to depart your puny planet and travel back to our own galaxy. MADRE DE DIOS! THE KLAXONS!'

An explosion tears the front doors off the shack.

FORTY TWO

The aliens run like scared women into the back of the shack as the shattered, burning remains of the doors fall down around our ears.

Sue's on it like a shot, peering around the wreckage of the threshold with the Uzi held high and ready. She signals a no-show and I pop out the cannon and head towards the entrance.

Nothing. Empty space. Sand. Dirt. Nothing for miles.

'Stick 'em up, mister.' The voice is high and squeaky. I look down and there's the Klaxon—just under a foot tall, small and plump, wrapped in a camouflage cape.

'What's the problem?'

'You're the problem, earth twat,' the Klaxon squeaks, and pokes me in the leg with his raygun.

I bend down and pick him up. He kicks and squirms for a few seconds and tries to take my head off with a few badly aimed shots, but Sue steps forward and takes the gun off him.

'Okay, small fry, give us the low-down,' I say, and give him a shake for good measure.

'This how you get your kicks?' the Klaxon shrieks. 'Picking on midgets!'

'Only alien midgets,' I tell him. 'As far as I'm concerned

you're messing with my case. I've been through the wringer over the last few hours and right now my patience is at an end. If you've got no beef with me then take a hike and bother some other gumshoe. If you have, state your case and we'll see if you can crawl your way out of a trashcan. Now spill the beans, stumpy.'

'Earthling bellend,' the Klaxon shrieks, 'I have no "beef" with you. Only *them!*' And he points a finger at the aliens.

I set the Klaxon down. 'Then we've got no problem,' I tell him.

The aliens snap their fingers and suddenly there's nothing but dust in the air. The Klaxon races outside into the summer heat, shimmers and disappears. I turn to Sue.

'Am I getting old or did I just imagine that?'

'Not unless we're both losing our minds.' But it's not a problem, as the shark's been fixed and the aliens have gone, and we're back on the road with a wave to Ginger.

'That was the single most unusual experience of my life,' says Sue, trailing her hand in the wind.

'Stick around,' I tell her, and the tractor beam hits us and we're up in the air and flying.

FORTY THREE

The Klaxons have us by the proverbial balls, and the view isn't pretty from up here. We're getting higher and higher and the ground's getting smaller.

'We need to plug what's holding us up,' I tell Sue. 'Keep an eye on the wheel.'

I let go and pull out the cannon, aiming straight up at the blue light that's shining down on us. But the Klaxons hang a right and their spaceship swings round, the tractor beam throwing us wide, screaming through the air without support and the ground coming up fast.

And what's worse, there's too much wind to light my smoke.

I turn and pop a shot into space where the ship once was, and now it's over us again. The tractor beam latches on to us and we're spinning and flying through the air. This is worse than being married.

'I've got an idea.' Sue aims the Uzi straight up and starts

firing at the ship. The bullets punch through the thin metal surface and smoke starts belching from what could be the engine.

'Lucky shot,' I tell her. 'But we're a mountain high in the air with nothing but hard earth beneath us. Whichever way you look at it, we could be in trouble.'

The Klaxons' spaceship stutters and sparks and the blue beam holding us up cuts out, and we're falling hard and fast. The craft explodes and a small capsule spirals down. Propellers pop out of the top, and the capsule starts buzzing about the car as we fall.

'Take a pot-shot, honey,' I say to Sue as I settle back into the driving seat. The ground's getting closer by the second. This is going to be messy. 'Might as well take out the space munchkin.'

She does, and the capsule sparks and explodes.

Just then another beam snatches us and we're floating again. This time more sedately.

'We have saved you, earthling filth,' booms the voice of Alien No. 1. 'In a matter of seconds we will land you safely on your earth soil to carry on your—'

And that's it. A beam splits their spaceship in half and it blossoms into a fireball. I look down to find the Klaxon hanging on the driver's door with an evil grin on its face and an ugly looking weapon in its hand.

'Game over, earth knob,' it manages, before I slam a fist into its pint sized head and send it hurtling into the abyss below.

'The jig is up.' Sue sits back in the seat with her arms along the backrest. 'We could have done with taking out Kieran.'

'You win some you lose some,' I mutter. Above us the Klaxon pops open an emergency chute on its backpack. Should have figured.

Except we don't hit the ground.

FORTY FOUR

We land on a soft airbag. I look over the side of the shark and we're on some sort of galleon. A huge, two hundred foot ship with sails and masts, riding on six massive wheels and powered by a huge turbo engine at the back. A couple of salty sea dog types walk suspiciously up to the car, swords and handguns drawn.

'Take me to your leader,' I mutter, and seconds later we're on the main deck staring into the eyes of some rugged shiny-toothed pirate, but without the eye patch.

'You the monkey in charge around here?' I snap open a cheroot and take a puff on the flame. 'You going anywhere near Kieran's compound? I assume you've heard of him, since every other joker in these parts seems to have a fixation on the loser.'

'Not on my watch, buddy,' says the pirate in straight edge Californian. 'We're totally pirates.'

'That's nice,' chips in Sue. 'We need to get off this rig.'

'Bain't none of that, missy,' chirrups a salty sea dog with a cutlass and an eyepatch, who's standing behind her. 'We aims to gizzard yer on the yard-arm.'

'Cut the crap, Long John,' I growl, turning on him. 'We've been through an earful of accents and we want out.' I whip the popgun out and aim straight for the captain's head. 'Now turn this war wagon around or I ventilate your captain.'

'Aha.' The captain smiles nervously and tentatively moves the barrel of the gun away from his face. 'That's totally radical, dude, but we've got, like, this total voyage to go on. Y'know, pillaging and suchlike. We're on a one way course, man.'

'Open to negotiation?' It's a small hope but anything's worth a try.

'We've got a headwind up, dude,' says the captain. 'Soon as it falls we'll drop you off. Hang loose, man.'

It's like being trapped in Hell, but without the laughs. The ship's full of scurvy old coves and laid back surfer dudes.

Sue snatches a few strands of info from the crew and fills in the story. 'They've got a feud running with the monks over the next mountain range,' she tells me. 'Something about a clash of theologies. I don't know the details, but their religions don't mix and they've decided to settle their differences with sword and gun. You ask me they're out of their minds, but what do I know?'

'And we're along for the ride, sister.' I glance around at the shark as the pirates lower the car off the crash mat we landed on. The captain comes over and throws an arm around my shoulders. 'Totally join us for breakfast, dude.' So we do.

FORTY FIVE

It's a good spread, and Sue tucks in like it's going out of fashion. I take a snifter of whisky and pour a few shots down to take the edge off the reality.

'I'd like you to touch base with my hombre, Hawkins,' says the captain, as an austere looking man walks into the cabin. He drags a chair out and sits down.

'I hear you fell from the sky,' he says, and I nod. 'Do you have any powers or magic you could trade with us?'

'No,' I say flatly, and knock back another shot. 'You live on a pirate ship that runs on wheels, Hawkins. Trust me, you don't need any help from us.'

'I believe you met a monk in another land,' says Hawkins. I can feel his eyes watching me, studying.

'We met more nuns than monks.' And this causes a stir. The captain's up on his feet with his hand on his single shot blunderbuss.

'Sit down, Tarnation,' coaxes Hawkins.

Tarnation sits with a mumbled 'Dude.'

'Tell us what you know of the nuns, for they are of much interest to us.' Hawkins sits exaggeratedly forwards.

'Your story, sister,' I nod to Sue.

'There's not much to tell,' says Sue, and she appears more reluctant than usual. 'They took me when I was young and had nowhere to go. They taught me in the arts of pottery and to believe in everlasting life. When I was old enough to think for myself, I hijacked a bishop and used his life to bargain my way out of trouble. Ever since then they've been after me.'

'Interesting,' notes Hawkins. 'But lies.'

The door bursts open and a salty sea dog runs in.

'Sir, the nuns are starboard bound, by god,' he coughs, with the fear of Hell in his eyes. 'We're all doomed, I tell 'ee!'

'Grab her!' yells Hawkins, and the sea dog is on Sue before I can pull the popgun out. When I look up the captain has the blunderbuss levelled straight at my head.

'We'll bargain with these two,' says Hawkins.

FORTY SIX

We're on the starboard bow facing an open topped double-decker London bus full of nuns who are baying for our blood.

A handful of sea dogs, tending towards over-salty, have us by the arms, waving cutlasses and firearms in the air and generally making a mess of things. The captain stands firm with Hawkins, but neither of them look comfortable.

'We have your charge!' shouts Hawkins at the Lead Nun. 'What will you bargain for her?'

'The opportunity not to tear your guts out and wear them as a vest!' yells the Lead Nun. 'You have no bargaining power with us, Pirate. You're godless heathens and you'll burn in the eternity of Hell. Even more so if you don't hand the bitch over!'

'We outnumber you ten to one!' yells Hawkins, but there's fear in his eyes. I guess he's never been threatened by a nun with an AK47 before.

'Your threats mean nothing but wasted air to us, Pirate!' bellows the Lead Nun, and she fires a few rounds into the side of the land galleon. Sea dogs scatter like the wind. 'Now hand her over before I tear you a new rectal passage and use your eyeballs as a pair of love blobs for my dog.'

'We have no choice,' whispers Hawkins to the captain, but I'm not standing for this.

'You've got every choice, Hawkins,' I snap, and he and the captain look at me in shame. 'You going to let a bus full of theologistic wimple knockers tell you how to live your life? I figured you for a shipful of heels the moment I smelled you.'

'You're going to bitch slap the monks *because* you clash in your religions, dammit!' yells Sue. 'What's the difference between the nuns and the monks? None! Now get your balls between your teeth and show these people just what being a pirate's all about.'

'Your words are sweet but those guns are aimed at our heads,' says Hawkins. 'And right now they're more persuasive than the bargaining skills of a lady, no matter how refined.'

There are two ways to resolve a dilemma like this. You either give up or fight your way out. And I'm all out of patience for these spineless sea dogs.

'You're a disgrace,' I snarl at Hawkins, and then jerk an elbow back into the sea dog who's holding me. He doubles up and I'm out with the cannon in a flash. 'Eat leaden death, penguin scum,' I shout, and blast the Lead Nun off the top deck of the double decker.

FORTY SEVEN

It's like a switch goes off in the pirates' heads. They yell and scream and cry 'victory' as the nuns start to spray the land galleon with bullets.

The man at the wheel spins a hard right and the galleon creaks and groans and swerves into the bus with a grinding crunch. Hawkins snaps out a blunderbuss and pops off smoke and flame at the bus. A nun goes down clutching her chest.

'Good shooting, Tex,' I tell him, and run across the deck to one of the cannons, hefting a ball into it and spinning it towards the bus.

I yank the firing string and the cannon belches fire, and the ball blasts a hole in the top deck. Nuns scatter into the air. It's like watching a monochrome whirlwind in action.

But the nuns are feisty. Years of ruler abuse and abstinence has bred a tribe strong enough to take on the world and still feel resentful. A cascade of AK fire tears up the starboard side of the galleon and sends splinters flying.

'Hawkins, get over here!' I yell, and Hawkins comes, blasting a nun off the bus as he runs.

'Your woman talks a good talk, but you walk the walk of a true hero,' he tells me.

'Thanks, but can it. We got a bus full of nuns to offload.'

I grab one side of the cannon and Hawkins grabs the other. A few of the sea dogs spot this and start to help, and in seconds we've got the cannon held high.

'Throw!' I yell, and they do it automatically before they can think about it. The cannon sails down and hits the ground, and the bus ploughs in to it. London Transport is no match for two tons of solid steel and wood. The cannon splinters, but the barrel holds and the bus starts to tip.

Penguins bail out over the sides as the double decker groans and goes over, landing with a shattering roar on the desert floor. The pirates cheer as a few remaining nuns fire off pot shots at the departing galleon.

'Suck my cloister, bitches!' yells the captain, then he turns to me with a smile. 'You have shown courage, my friend. But what can we do for you as repayment?'

'Take us back to the road,' I tell him. 'Set us on our way.'

'Alas, we cannot,' says Hawkins, with genuine regret. Then, 'Clap them in irons.'

FORTY EIGHT

We're chained up below decks and Sue's not looking happy. 'We should have gone with the nuns,' she moans. 'We would have had a better chance.'

'I wouldn't trust those nuns with a bible,' I tell her. 'Now keep tight and quiet and I'll get us out of here.'

The cell door opens and Hawkins walks in with a big smile on his face.

'We've reached an agreement,' he says. 'You help us fight the monks and we'll take you back to the road. It's either that or we slit your gizzards right here and now.'

'Is there a third option?' I ask.

'No,' says Hawkins, and the door slams shut.

Time passes and I watch through the porthole as dusk falls. And in the distance the monastery approaches through the night. It's lit by torches, and a deep, low chanting is coming from inside the walls. I recognise it.

FORTY NINE

The tomb of the ancient warrior. Except it isn't a tomb. It's a huge edifice built to withstand the swords of a hundred thousand warriors, and it stretches up into the sky. And these pirate jokers haven't got a clue what they're in for. Hawkins drags us up to the bow of the ship and points at the building.

'Splice the main brace and do something nautical!' yells one of the pirates. 'If we pull this off we'll live like kings!'

A yell goes up from the crew. Hawkins leans close to me. 'I'm going to cut you loose, but there's something you have to do for me.'

'Fire away.'

'In the basement stands a rank, terrible demon. Dispose of it and I'll reward you beyond your wildest dreams. I know you have power over such creatures. Legend has spoken of it.'

'Whatever you say, Hawkins.' And the ropes are off and the cannon is back in my hand.

The edifice looms up out of the darkness and the walls are lined with a thousand armed guards. The odds are stacked against us, but anyone who can beat off a busload of nuns is worth their weight in bullets.

'Attack!' screams Hawkins, and the land galleon ploughs into the monastery and tears a hole through the wall. The pirates stream over the sides and into the building and it's every man for himself.

But I'm staying out of this one. This isn't my fight. Bodies are falling left, right and centre as I stroll through the carnage, taking time to admire some of the ancient architecture. I strike a match on the beard of a passing warrior.

'We should be fighting!' Sue looks panicked.

'We've got no disagreement with these people.' I wave her off. 'We've got a basement to go to.'

Behind us pirates clash with armed guards, gunshots go off, bodies flail and the blood flies. I open the basement door and a huge winding column of steps leads us down into the smoky darkness. Halfway down I see the head. All smoke and fire. Blazing red eyes. A demon as big as the building.

'Hi, Bob,' I say. 'Somebody wants you dead.'

'They always do,' sighs Bob. 'Can you believe the racket they're making.'

'The joker in charge wants me to banish you back to the netherworld. I think he's barking up the wrong reality.'

Bob shifts around to face me and the building trembles. 'I didn't get a chance to thank you.'

'It's not necessary,' I tell him. 'Did you get your balls back?'

'A little bruised,' says Bob with a half smile. 'That was one hell of a kick you gave Steps. I never should have let him trick me. One moment he's whispering sweet glory into your ear and the next he's got your balls.' Bob shakes his head. 'Bad state of affairs.'

'He shrink 'em?'

Bob nods. 'Shrank them, took them, glued them on and used their power for his own.' Bob smiles. 'But that's okay. I've got them back now. These suckers aren't going anywhere.'

'Where's Chicago?' I ask.

'Right behind you, tough guy.' I turn and Chicago's there with a smile. 'We got some bother. Want to help us out? We can pull a switch.'

'Forget the switch, Chicago. Just let Bob loose on them.'

'I have forsaken all violence,' says Bob.

'Flip a coin?' I suggest, and he does, and I win.

FIFTY

Hawkins is on the deck as the battle rages before him. I walk up to him with Sue in tow.

'Problem solved, Hawkins. Basically, you need to get the hell out of here or you and your crew will end up on the wrong side of dead.'

But he isn't listening. He strides to the front of the galleon. 'All bow down to our gods and there shall be peace!' And suddenly there's a cowled figure beside him, face hidden by shadow. It's Chicago.

'We can all live in harmony together as one,' comes the voice from the cowl.

'Not by our ways, cowled dog,' snarls Hawkins. 'Ye all be worthless to me. I'll see you walk the plank before I see our two religious beliefs join hands.'

'Fair enough,' shrugs the figure, then it turns to me. 'Coming with us, Joe?'

'Stand me a smoke and something wet and I'll fill in the details.'

'No problem,' nods Chicago, and a gigantic clawed hand punches out from the ground under the galleon. Chicago snaps his fingers and the next moment we're on the battlements as the pirate galleon gets pulled down into the earth. I see Hawkins shaking a fist at me and yelling something incomprehensible as he's sucked down to Hell.

'These morons'll never learn,' laughs Chicago. 'Smoke?'

I snap one of my own alight and he leads me down the hallway.

'I've got a problem,' he tells me. 'Only you can solve it. We've got something big, mean and ugly in the top tower and it's refusing to budge.'

'Just send Bob in to sort it out,' I suggest.

'Bob won't go near it.' Chicago turns a corner and stops at the bottom of a flight of steps that lead up towards a bright, shining light. 'Says if he goes anywhere near it the world ends, and the son-of-a-bitch won't listen to me. I don't believe him. I just think he's afraid. I know what's up there, and it's more powerful than anything the ruler of Hell could deal with. Maybe even more powerful than Kieran.'

'Let me guess. It's God up there.'

'Worse than that.' Chicago shoots me a doleful look. 'It's Norman Mailer. And he's brought Hemingway and Huston for a party.' This is worse than I thought.

FIFTY ONE

Sue wants to come, but I tell her to keep back and wait for me with the Uzi. If they come down the stairs then we'll need all the help we can get. As I walk up the steps I spare a glance back at the monastery laid out below. The whole place is tooled up and ready for action, but I know it's not enough. Guns can't stop these people.

As I get near the top of the staircase the light gets brighter and the noise grows louder. I don't bother knocking, I just kick the door open.

Mailer's the first to spot me. He laughs and throws me a bottle of whisky. Good stuff.

'Joe Fury,' he says, and takes a puff from his enormous cigar. 'As I live and breathe. Still fighting against the American Dream?'

'That was always your bag, Mailer,' I tell him. Huston's playing around with his monkey and Hemingway's dousing his throat with a good kick of rum. 'What the hell are you old farts doing sparking out in the same place?'

'We came to offer you advice, my boy,' says Huston. 'We've been keeping a close eye on your travels and we know the kind of difficulty you've been up against.'

'If it's that difficult, ditch the afterlife and lend me a hand.'

I settle back into a wickerwork chair and light up the Cuban Hemingway hands me. 'With the four of us in there we could knock this hustler into shape.'

'If only that were so, my boy,' says Huston. 'If only. But we're out of action, I'm afraid. Our time has passed and we can only offer you support and advice.'

'No offence, but that's about as much use as an empty bottle.' I drain the whisky and throw it aside. Mailer hands me another.

'Chicago tried to pull some strings with the Forces of Nature, but nothing gives, Fury.' Mailer looks sad and angry. 'I couldn't reason with them either, so I took a pop at them. Nothing the Forces of Nature hate more than getting a right hook in the kisser.'

'Let's face it, Fury,' says Hemingway. 'With our reputations we couldn't scrape shit from a barrel as a favour to Nature. So we're stuck on the sidelines.'

'No sweat, Papa.' I raise the bottle in salute. 'Just good to see you again. I got a major concern, though. What can you tell me about the dame?'

'Don't trust her,' snaps Mailer. 'She doesn't quote on our radar. We don't know where she's from or what she's done.'

'Don't over-react, Mailer,' says Huston, and he turns to me. 'It's true, we don't know a thing about her. We know her past is a mystery, and we know it's mixed up tight with Kieran.'

'Spare me the newsflash, Huston,' I tell him.

'Now, I know you know this, but you should also consider how much we don't know about her.' Huston taps the side of his head for emphasis. 'If she doesn't turn up on our radar then she's neither good nor bad. You understand me, boy?'

'How come?'

'We hear things where we are,' says Huston. 'Whispers, words, a few rumours and the odd spark of speculation. None of it's concrete as individual items, but they all tie up once they're put together. No facts, though. Facts are not to be trusted. Instinct is.'

'That dame's saved my ass more than once,' I tell them, but somehow I understand they already know this. 'The option of ditching her is non-existent. Now what do you know about Kieran that could help the case?'

'Don't touch him,' says Mailer. 'Everyone who touches him falls under his spell. Why do you think he gets his fingers in so many pies?'

'He knows everyone and anyone,' says Hemingway. 'He's everywhere. You think of a scheme and he's already done it. He lives in every lifetime and every moment in somebody's life. At least, that's what he likes to think.'

'And there we have our weakness,' says Huston with a smile. 'His ego could be the end of him. Now, I don't know how or why or when or where, but somehow his destiny could be tied up with the size of his ego. You see a grand-standing ego like his and it adds weight to a man's soul. It ties him down. Our collective egos could bring down a mountain—Kieran likes to think he *is* the mountain. Do you see what I'm saying, Fury?'

'Cut out the cryptic shenanigans and we might be talking.' I slip a pack of Cubans into my top pocket and spin the cap on a fresh whisky. 'I need something concrete.'

'But that's the problem,' says Huston. 'That's what we can't explain. There *is* nothing concrete. Just rumours. Whispers. Hearsay.'

'Puncture the ego and you could be in business,' says Mailer. 'But we hear through the grapevine that he's got something big in the pipeline, so you can't hang around.'

'Immovability,' says Huston with a smile. 'Just remember that. Immovability.'

I drink long and hard from the whisky and throw it back to Huston. 'Thanks, old man.'

'Now go,' he says, and I leave the three of them laughing, drinking and smoking.

The door slams behind me. Their words don't mean much, but they've sparked off a few plans in my head.

Then someone hits me from behind and the world goes black. And when I wake up I'm in Paris.

FIFTY TWO

I get up and spot Sue on a chair by a table that's propping up a few margaritas. We're by the Seine, and Sue's dolled up in a light gown and a sun hat, wearing shades.

She smiles warmly and picks up a margarita.

'Come on, Joe, join me,' she says. 'Take the breeze off your feet.'

I stagger over and sit down, feeling the back of my neck. There's a lump.

'How'd this happen?' I ask her, and she shrugs.

'Who cares. The drinks are free.'

I sip a drink. Doesn't taste like a Mickey Finn. I down the whole thing to be sure and wait. Nothing unusual.

'You just woke up and this was this, yeah?' Somehow I don't buy into it.

Sue smiles behind the sunglasses and looks out over the Seine. 'It is a beautiful day, Joe Fury. Somehow the shallow existence of life seems such a treasure. We could while away the rest of our eternity in such mediocre pleasure.'

'What the hell are you talking about, doll?' I mutter. 'They drug you?'

'Ah, Joe Fury, you talk such a funny way.' And Sue giggles. And something about it sends chills down my spine. 'We are merely the future of our family's regret. We must laugh when we can. And we must cry . . . when we can't.'

'They take the Uzi off you?' But she's not paying attention.

'The past is not important to us, Mr Fury,' she laughs playfully. 'The past is full of regrets which can only hold us back. I want to run and sing and dance with the life I hold inside of me. Come with me, Fury. Come with me to the ends of the earth and never look back.'

'Snap out of it, toots,' I tell her. 'You're raving like a madwoman.'

'Madness is merely a state of mind,' she dribbles, and this is enough for me. I get up and start walking for the nearest alley. Something fishy about this whole charade.

I reach the alleyway and it's flat. Cardboard. We're on some kind of film set and somehow they've taken the guts out of Sue.

'Sue, get over here and stop drinking that poison!' She giggles, kicks her feet, and scampers over.

'This life is so . . . outré,' she says, and slumps playfully against my arm.

'Take a step back, doll, this could be nasty.' And I pull back a fist and slam it straight through Paris.

FIFTY THREE

Paris falls around us, crashing down to reveal nothing but a deep, dark dungeon stretching out into the infinite.

'If this is Paris, then we're up the creek,' I mutter.

'It is but the darkness in my soul,' chitters Sue, and starts to totter off. I lay a hand on her shoulder and she stops.

'Better let me make the tracks, sister,' I tell her. 'Even if they took my cannon I still got these.' I whip out a Cuban and snap a light to the end of it. 'Let's go.'

I take a few steps into the dungeon and come up sharp against a solid object. I rap on it and it's the darkness painted onto balsa wood.

I give the wood a shove and the walls fall down, and we're knee deep in the jungle with birdcalls and sunlight blazing down through the thick canopy overhead.

'This is some kind of joke,' I say to myself, because nothing's sinking through Sue's skull as she flits and giggles through the cardboard grass.

She scampers up to a plastic fawn and slams headfirst into a cardboard tree, which topples into the background. The next layer falls to present the fires of Hell rendered in glorious balsa.

After a drag on the Cuban I stride forward and knock a fist through Hell. Next we get New York in the 1830's. After that a distant blue planet full of crystal trees. After that some guy with a cigarette on the go is yakking at a guy called Blakey by some balsa wood buses. I punch through wall after wall and scenario after scenario, until finally I crash through into a stark white room.

A low hum fills the room. Sue finally puts a gag on the philosophising. And a steel wall slams shut behind us where the balsa wood displays once stood.

'Congratulations, Mister Fury,' booms a deep, sonorous voice. 'You have finally reached the object of your destiny. Now look upon my works, ye mighty, and fear me!'

FIFTY FOUR

Except there's nothing. Empty space and clean white walls. No doors—just a sheet of cloth hanging against the far wall.

'Okay, wiseguy,' I say. 'What's the big idea?'

'You wanted a meeting with me, Mr Fury, and here I am.'

'All I see is an OCD room. I don't see anyone.'

'All that matters is that I can see you,' says the voice, and I twig who it is.

'Kieran?'

'That's right,' booms the voice of Kieran, and the sound of galloping horses fills the air. It's meant to be psychologically disorientating but it's nothing but cheap parlour tricks to me.

'Okay, cut the crap,' I yell over the noise, and the sound cuts out immediately. 'Nice place. Love to stick around. Why don't we talk about this man to man?'

'I'm not open to bribes, Mr Fury,' booms the voice of Kieran. 'But I *am* open to intellectual debate.'

I finger the popgun under my jacket. 'There's plenty of time for talk. Let's grab a snifter and chat about how we can resolve this matter. I can appreciate you don't want to be taken in, so let's talk.'

'We are.'

'Face to face.' This is getting us nowhere. I snap a glance at Sue and she nods. Back to normal.

'What are the basic tenets of existence?' booms the voice. I've had enough of this.

'Your call, toots.' Sue nods at me and steps forward into the middle of the room, ready to take on the intellectualisation. I start scouring the walls for any signs of an escape. Hidden lever, switch—anything. I tear back the cloth on the far wall. Smooth surface and nothing else.

'The basic tenets of existence are "shut your ass and get your fat face down here, pig fucker!"' She's got moxy, but it's not the right answer.

'Always a disappointment, Suzanne,' the voice mocks. 'So smart and yet so dumb.'

'Kiss my hairy ass, dickface!' She's really getting into it, and it's keeping his highness distracted. 'You're about as intellectual as a kick in the maracas. You can't fool me.'

'I took so much time and effort with you, Suzanne.' But somehow the voice doesn't sound too bothered. 'You could have been in line to take over my position once the ultimate plan had been officiated.'

'Always talking a bagful of air, aren't we, Kieran.' She's defiant. Whatever he's done to her, I'd hate to be his testicles once she gets a hold of them. 'Let's try some smarts, Kieran. What are the basic building blocks of life?'

'A random camel in a telephone factory!' The volume suddenly ramps up and the air booms and shrieks with monkey sounds. He's back on the old mental wavelength again, and I can't find a way out.

'We could be stuck here, sister.' I turn to Sue. 'No exit.'

'If I know Kieran, there's an exit,' says Sue.

'Watch out for the flying sheep, Mr Fury,' Kieran shrieks. 'They are coming for you, and you alone.'

'I can't wait to plug this guy,' I mutter to Sue. And then we hear the noise. A steam train. Whistle. Engine. Getting closer and closer.

Sue whips back the cloth hanging over the wall and suddenly the smooth wall is gone and there's a hole the size of a door with a railway track leading right towards us. And at the end of the railway track an ancient steam locomotive is heading in our direction.

I pull out the popgun. 'This could get messy.'

'It's one of his tricks.' Sue turns and heads for the wall opposite, then starts tapping on it all over.

'Hurry it up, toots,' I yell over my shoulder. 'This could be the end of a beautiful relationship.'

'Stow it, Fury.' She's concentrating. 'I've got a job to do.'

I turn back to the train. No way out of this one. The floor starts to shake. As I turn back Sue knocks the very base of the wall and a door pops open.

'This way.'

Too late. The train slams into the room, punching me backwards. I fly through the door, grabbing Sue as I pass, and fall into an eternal blackness.

FIFTY FIVE

An eternal blackness which lasts about thirty seconds before we hit the ground. It's daylight. I get up, brush myself down, and help the dame up. Nothing but rocky outcrops around us.

Then: 'Halt, stranger!' I spin around and there's some dame

in a skimpy outfit and knee high boots holding a popgun. 'What do you know of the evil Count Zarth Arn and his ultimate weapon?'

'Depends on who's asking,' I say, brushing myself down.

'I am Stella Star, and I am sent by my people to defeat the Count.' She stands straight haughtily, flicking her hair back. I could get to like a woman like this.

'That's just peachy, toots.' I glance around. Nothing of interest. 'Which way out of this joint?'

'I know what this is,' Sue whispers to me. 'Stella! Where is your robot companion, Elle?'

'He is gathering fuel pods for our fighter,' says Stella with another haughty flick. Seems to be her stock in trade.

'You won't get any help from her,' says Sue. 'She doesn't exist.'

FIFTY SIX

'Okay, sister, mind explaining what the hell that was all about?' We're walking away from the woman and out into an endless sea of sand and rocks. It's like being back home.

'I don't think I can explain it,' says Sue. 'Kieran told me about it. People think things up and they become reality. All the thoughts and ideas laid down crop up somewhere in some alternate universe or something like that. It had a lot to do with quantum physics, but I'm not exactly sure what.'

'Multiple earth theory.' I fill her in on the details. 'Thought up by some schmo called William James. It posits that anything and everything can happen, or something like that. We just split off into alternate realities when it does happen.' I snap a light and spark a cheroot.

'If we're here then we have to get back,' says Sue, looking around. 'Any ideas.'

'Yeah, watch out,' I push her out of the way as a giant lizard-like creature explodes out of the earth between us, like a huge worm with teeth. It slams down into the ground and twitches around to face us.

No defence against Joe Fury's popgun. I put a bullet right in the cortex and it writhes and convulses and undulates and then decides to take a nap.

'Close call, sister.' But when I get up and look around she's not there. And I'm in a graveyard.

FIFTY SEVEN

And it's night. And there appears to be a horde of zombies heading in my direction, with my face on the menu.

'Tough call.' I take a puff on the stoogie and look for an exit. In the distance, a giant shopping mall.

It takes a good hour to get there, but the living dead are slow and stupid. When I reach it I bang on the door and nothing happens. Behind me the zombies are starting to make their presence known.

I turn the popgun towards them and aim for the nearest head. 'Say hello to poppa,' I mutter, and squeeze off a shot. But the zombie ducks, and then looks up, confused.

'What's the big idea, mac?' This is a turn up for the books.

'Take one chunk out of me and you're history.' I cock the gun for emphasis.

'We *are* history, ya moron!' yells another zombie—a dead cop.

'Can it, flatfoot,' I yell back. 'I know your M.O.'

A tall, astute looking zombie clears a path through the crowd. It's wearing a cravat and holds a cigarette in a long stemmed filter.

'Why, my dear boy, you have been completely misled by your prejudices,' says the creature. 'My name's Tarquin, and if you'll come with me I can fill you in on the details.'

FIFTY EIGHT

I'll say this about the living dead—they know how to keep a house in order.

Tarquin sits opposite me in a leather chair while I nurse a shot of bourbon.

'We have been a much maligned and feared race throughout the centuries,' says Tarquin. He speaks like an English lord. 'The legends and superstitions associated with us over the years have led people to believe we are blood-thirsty creatures, whose only compulsion is munching on the living and possibly eating their brains if the feeling takes us. But I say, "a pox on that".'

'Your ear's coming off,' I tell him, and he jams it back into place.

'Thank you.' Tarquin readjusts himself in the seat. 'But you do not need to shoot us in the head to get the best out of us. We were once like you. Civilised.'

'Now you're getting nasty.' I reach for the popgun under my jacket but Tarquin waves me away.

'You can drop the pretence now, Mr Fury,' he says. 'We're all the same under the skin.'

'The difference is I can see your liver,' I tell him, and shoot back the bourbon. 'Hey, I'm all for equal rights, but I've got a job to do and I need to do it now. I've lost the main squeeze and there's a rat that needs taking down. I need to get on with the case.'

'You'll have plenty of time for that, Mr Fury.' And I don't like the tone of his voice. I throw down the empty glass and get up, spinning around with the gun out.

FIFTY NINE

And find I'm in a land of too many colours. There's a big, yellow road leading off into the distance and some morons singing and dancing at the end of it.

I turn to find a whole bunch of pixies stretching their legs and lighting up.

'Jesus, thank god she's gone,' says the nearest one. 'If that bloody woman had opened her mouth one more bloody time, I'd have vomited up my spleen!'

'Tell me about it,' says some woman dressed like a fairy, but with a voice straight out of Brooklyn. She scratches her rear, then sparks up a cigar bigger than her head and continues necking a litre of whisky. 'Anything to get rid of the bitch.'

'Heads up, ladies, I need some advice.' I step into their frame. They spare me a glance and then get back to their bitching.

'If she comes back we'll stick her in the wicker man,' says one of the pixies.

'You'll do no such thing!' booms a voice behind me.

I turn to find some guy in a police uniform smoking a joint, two young ladies hanging off his arms and caressing his hairy chest. I'm not on the yellow road any more, but a huge windswept hill surrounded by hippies.

'If there's any burning to be done around here it's going to be done by me!' The flatfoot nods to a small crowd, who pick up a tall guy dressed as a woman and heft him towards a huge wicker man.

'How do you like them apples, you big girl's blouse!' booms the flatfoot, and he reduces the joint to ash in one draw. He turns to me. 'Hello, boyo.'

'Who's the chick?' I nod to the man-woman as he screams and struggles. His captors throw him into the wicker man and lock the door behind him.

'You're looking for Kieran, aren't you now, boy?' booms the flatfoot, and I'm starting to guess he's got no other form of communication.

'You could say that.' I drop the stoogie and crush it out. 'I'm looking for the hard and fast way, and right now I'm getting sidetracked.'

'Oh, you don't have to worry about that, boyo. Just stick it through, yes? This is a test, you see?'

'I gave up tests when I got kicked out of school,' I snarl. 'Any advice?'

'Yes. Watch out!'

And I turn to see a huge swarm of bees heading straight towards me.

SIXTY

The hill's been replaced by what looks like the centre of a small village. An English drunk in a safari suit grabs me.

'Move yer bladdy self!' he shouts, and drags me into a store. 'Jesus, man, don't you even know when the killer bees are coming? It's been all over the bladdy news.'

'Now, that's no way to treat a man, Peachy!' The voice is Scottish. I turn, and we're on a windswept mountain. The drunk and the Scotsman are dressed in furs, and both are smiling and smoking.

'This part of the test?'

'Test it may be, but it is of no interest to us,' says the Scotsman. 'Me and Peachy are willing to put a wager on with you.' He holds out his hand. 'My name's Danny.'

'Joe Fury.' I shake his hand. 'What's the wager?'

'Well, me and Peachy here are looking to take over Kafiristan, and we need some help. We were wondering if you were up for the adventure. For the sake of a mother's son.'

'Going to the east, etcetera, etcetera.' I turn to Peachy. 'Yeah, I know the drill and I'm not part of the clan, so count me out if that's a precondition. Kafiristan's out of my district, and I need to get back on the case, so excuse me if I decline, gentleman. I've got a job to do.'

'We all do, Fury,' says a voice behind me, but I'm not surprised. Kieran's tactics involve subterfuge.

I turn, and a guy in a trenchcoat and trilby stands in front of me sparking a cigarette. He shakes the match out and gives me the visual once over with a crooked smile.

'You looking for a way out?' asks the man.

'Could be,' I say. 'Got something I can use?'

'Depends on what you know.' The figure steps forward, one hand in his pocket. I can tell he's packing.

'Let's cut the jousting,' I tell him. 'We'll play it fair and square. I'm looking for—'

'Yeah, yeah.' He waves me away. 'I know the drill and I'm tired of hearing it. We're both stuck in the same routine. Chances are you got some info you can give me. I heard a rumour on the docks that you've got a watch. A very valuable watch. Something a man like me could use in a tight spot.'

'You hear all kinds of things.'

'I can bargain with you,' says the man. 'Give me the watch and I'll get you a one way ticket out of this joint.'

'I'm not up for bargaining,' I tell him.

'I like your style.' He smiles. 'But the truth is we're fighting for the same side and only I can help you, so cough it up and we'll negotiate the terms later.'

'For a small man you've got a big mouth.'

He gets angry in a second and lunges for me. I give him a few quick slaps—left and right—and he's down on the floor. I snap his wallet out and go through it, pulling out his business card.

'Private eye, eh?' I throw the card down next to him. 'Well, Mr Spade, try growing a few inches and we'll talk about it.'

'Ya goddamn penis loving mutie!' he shrieks, and the mask falls off. This isn't Spade, but suddenly I'm not in the room anyway.

SIXTY ONE

I'm back in the white room and the guy on the floor is thrashing around like he's having a fit. There's a wide open door leading to the road, but the only problem is there's no sign of Sue.

'We'll get you, Fury,' shrieks the pint sized private eye. 'You're ours for the taking. Kieran will hunt you down and find you, and then you'll be nothing but a stain on the footnote of history.'

'Laugh it up, shorty,' I tell him, and step over the body and out of the building. The road is hot and dry and there's a butler standing nearby with a cold whisky and a Cuban on a silver tray.

'The master sends his best,' says the butler.

'Kieran?'

'The very same.' The butler hands me the whisky and I pick up the Cuban and light it. 'He wishes you a safe journey, but wonders if you might possibly help him out?'

'After what he's put me through? Is he crazy?'

'Quite possibly, sir,' says the butler, and then gestures to the shark nestling at the side of the road. Two life size porcelain figurines sit on the back seat—one black and one white. 'They're friends of his. They just need a lift to the nearest petrol station and then you can be on your way.'

'Thanks, Jeeves, but you can tell your master I don't take hitch-hikers.'

'He said you'd say that.' Jeeves pulls out one half of a note from his pocket and hands it over. I open it. It reads 'LOOK.' 'He says to inform you that the other half of the note is at the next petrol station along the road. He says to tell you it's a vital clue to the end of the mystery you have been embroiled in. And, by the way, Preston is waiting for you at the next juncture.'

SIXTY TWO

None of this adds up. Now Kieran is helping me and Preston's waiting. Sue has gone and the nuns are everywhere. Kieran's obviously got control of the whole state of reality around these parts. Which is probably why Preston wants him put away.

But none of that matters. I've got two hitch-hikers in the back of the car. They sit, staring ahead, and it doesn't take a genius to figure out they're the physical embodiment of Yin and Yang.

'So who's who?' I ask.

'I'm Yin,' says the black figure.

'Which makes you Yang,' I say to the white figure, and get no response.

'Have you ever considered the morality of what you're do-ing?' asks Yin.

'Have you ever considered keeping your mouth shut?' After the last few problems I'm in no mood for cod philosophising.

'The world is encompassed in light and dark,' says Yin. 'We live together as one in unity. Without conflict there could be no peace, and without Kieran there could be no quest.'

'Your status in the escapade is nothing but a grain of sand in a desert,' says Yang. 'You believe yourself to be on a case, to hold the key in your pocket to the capture of Kieran, and yet you are wholly unaware of your own position within the grand scheme of things.'

'All I know is that I've got a job to do, Preachy,' I tell him over my shoulder. 'Now can it!'

'You believe yourself to be the centre of the universe—that functionality cannot progress without you,' says Yang. 'You understand yourself in your own reality game plan to be the sole progenitor of all your thoughts, ideas, pasts and fu-tures, and yet you are blind to the understanding that reality is crafted from what the majority wish themselves to believe it is.'

'Kieran can offer you an alternative,' says Yin. 'Kieran can pull back the veneer which you believe to be what you perceive around you, and teach you how to manipulate what others believe to be their state of mind.'

'For the physical embodiment of the duality of nature and

how they're both intertwined you talk a lot of crap,' I tell them. 'I don't bargain. Kieran comes with me. End of story.'

'We are not your enemy,' says Yin. 'We are not your friend. We simply are.'

'You're Kieran's stooges.'

'Far from it,' says Yang. 'We are yet another facet of this fragile existence which has been chosen for us by extraneous forces. Yet we see the world around us as an indefinite thing. A brittle framework we wish to coalesce into the information we perceive. It's something you should contemplate, Mr Fury, lest you cease to exist as a fragment of our imaginings.'

'You guys must be fun at parties.'

'You would do well to remember that you are not the centre of the universe,' they say in unison. 'But merely a fragment in the stream of existence.'

The gas station looms up in the distance and puts an end to the multi-layered levels of bullshit these two are putting me through. We pull up and Yin and Yang are suddenly not in the car any more. As I step out of the shark I spot them in the diner, sitting by the window in a booth, facing each other.

Preston sits in the shadows. I can tell it's him by the wig.

SIXTY THREE

'No nuns?' I ask, and he shakes his head. I sit down across from him. 'What do you want?' I say.

'I want the girl,' says Preston, and his face is hard and set like stone.

'If I could find the girl I wouldn't hand her over anyway,' I tell him. 'You've pushed this out too far, Preston.'

'I can get you into Kieran's compound,' says Preston. 'I can bring you to him.'

'Give me the history,' I tell him.

'The history always changes,' says Preston. 'It depends on who's telling it. As for me, there is no history, just an endless series of coincidences that somehow wind up in the same order. Before me there were others, and when I'm gone—'

'Cut the crap, Preston,' I tell him. 'Just give me the facts. No, forget it, I've had enough of the facts. I need to get back on the road.'

Preston starts to protest, but it's too late. I'm up and out of the seat.

'I can help you,' pleads Preston, all pretence of the tough guy gone. 'I just need the watch.'

'Everyone needs the watch.' I walk over to Yin and Yang.

'We have devolved as we have evolved,' says Yin.

'Yeah, yeah.' I wave away his platitudes. 'You can tell Kieran that I only deal face to face. Tell him to ditch the philosophical, social and metaphysical crap and stop sending me his patsies to bargain with. I only work one way, and that's my way.'

'Kieran follows his own path,' they say in unison. 'As we follow ours.'

They're automatons. I wander over to the fridge and open the door, and see Sue hunched up inside of it, blinking against the light.

'Where have you been?' she asks, and then: 'Never mind. Look, we've got a problem. The sheep are after us.'

'Don't tell me, they fly?' I say, and she nods, grabs me, and pulls me into the fridge.

SIXTY FOUR

We fall for a few seconds and hit a wet, cold street. Huge tower blocks rear up on either side of us.

Sue doesn't seem concerned. She's up and out with the Uzi in a second.

'Let me guess,' she says. 'Preston was in there with you, and he was starting to spout a barrelful of pseudo-personal bullshit, correct?'

'You've hit the nail on the head, sister.' I get up and pull out the cannon.

'He's entering stage two psychosis,' she explains. 'It's what happens when you hang out with Kieran too much. You start to literally crawl up your own ass. *Here they come!*'

And with the sound of a heavy prop engine and demonic bleating the sky fills with row after row of fluffy white sheep. But these sheep have giant wings sprouting from their sides.

They peel off and start heading for us, bullets blazing from the guns in their wings.

I fire off a shot, taking one right in the goggles, then we're running, tearing down the street as bullets churn into the ground around us.

'Genetic mutations!' screams Sue. She spins and sweeps with the Uzi, taking off the wing of one of the flying sheep. The engine coughs and belches black smoke and then explodes, sending the bleating animal down to the earth.

'Kieran's?' I yell, taking out another ovine attacker.

'Not this one,' yells Sue, and drags me into a doorway as bullets chew up the pavement behind us. 'Professor Spanner. He used to work for Kieran. Unlike Teffle he's not one of the good guys.'

'So why is he after us?' I yell, popping out and emptying the cannon at one of the sheep. It dips, spins, barrels out of a slide and screams down towards us, wing-guns blazing.

'For Kieran's honour,' says Sue as the sheep approaches, its face set in a look of grim determination. She steps out and blasts the thing full in the face and it veers away, flips over and comes crashing to the ground with a strangled 'baah' of existential misery.

'And for the fun of it,' she says with a smile, and then she's out and running. I pitch in after her, reloading the cannon as I go. Behind us the phalanx of sheep slide in for a second run.

'Hold on,' says Sue, and pulls a small bag of grenades out from under her jumper. 'Watch this.'

Sue pulls the pin on a grenade and waits. The sheep stream in closer, bullets ricocheting off the ground and walls around us. One slices straight through the end of the cigar I've got in my mouth and lights the tip.

Sue lobs the grenade high into the air.

'Good time to get down,' she says.

The grenade flies dead centre into the mass of sheep, and it's carnage. When the explosion dies down there's nothing but wool and goggles falling from the sky.

'Eat my grenade,' says Sue, after the fact. Then the ground shakes.

'I've got a reasonably wary feeling about this,' she says, and turns. 'Oh dear.'

SIXTY FIVE

'I am Molesto, the King of the Sheep!' booms the seventy foot creature. It stands on its hind legs, almost wedged between the buildings, staring down at us with pure hatred. *'Who dares disturb my slumber?'*

'Joe Fury,' I snap, levelling the popgun. 'Take a hike back to the mint sauce factory.'

That doesn't go down well with Molesto. He roars and rears back, eyes flashing a deep red. I grab Sue and wrench her out of the way as two laser beams shoot from his pupils and blow a chunk out of the pavement.

'You got another fridge out of here?' I ask her, and she pulls out a map and starts to run a finger down it.

I step out in front of the giant sheep.

'Let's negotiate,' I yell, and the creature stops for a second. *'What do you have to offer?'*

'You've got to ask yourself, "what does a sheep like me want from a life like this?"' I'm stalling for time and glance back at Sue. She's still looking. 'And "what does a sheep with my personality want to gain in life?"'

'A fast car and a nice pair of shoes!' roars the sheep.

'I can understand that,' I say. 'But that kind of luxury doesn't get handed to you on a plate. You have to work for it.'

'Got it!' Sue stabs the map.

'And what do you suggest?' roars Molesto.

'Here's my first piece of advice.' I whip out the popgun and start blazing away, putting a few stretch marks in the giant sheep, but doing little else.

And we're off and running as the sheep roars in fury behind us and starts thundering down the street. Sue grabs me and yanks me into a doorway, and we burst through into a living room.

Molesto starts hammering away at the building, smashing his hooves into the brickwork, trying to tear it down around our ears.

Sue drags me into the kitchen where the fridge is. She pulls open the door and we're staring into the deep, empty blackness inside.

'Here goes nothing,' she says, and she's in. I pause for a

second to relight the Cuban in my mouth, then I follow, and
I'm tumbling through an endless blackness.

SIXTY SIX

I can feel something happening to my mind. It's like black
fingers are seeping into my consciousness and telling me to
give up the cheroots and whisky and start contemplating the
meaning of existence.

We're floating in black space and I can see Sue's straining
against her own problems.

'I ... I should wear frilly dresses and think about kittens,'
she gasps. 'No, dammit. Must fight!'

And I know what she means. The notion of buying a small,
economical foreign car enters my mind and I suddenly like the
idea of slippers.

'What's happening to us?'

'Fight it!' screams Sue, and then we're out of the blackness
and spilling onto a cold, hard metal floor.

'Congratulations, mein liege,' comes a voice, and I look up
to see a man in a white surgeon's gown—holding a scalpel—
standing over me.

'Professor Spanner, I presume?' I ask, and he just smiles.

SIXTY SEVEN

'So, vot do you think of my vortex of ultimate displeasure?'
asks the Professor, walking back and forth in front of us.

We're in the middle of a lab, the place stuffed full of curios
and scientific instruments.

'I think it could do with some improvement, Einstein,' I
snap. 'Nothing bags me out of a cigar and a shot, you understand me?'

'Hoh, yes, I understand you,' cackles the Prof. 'But unless
I am very much mistaken, you do not understand what kind of
trouble you are in.'

'My right fist says you're lying,' I say, and take a step towards him. He recoils, then cackles to himself.

'You are one of those hard men who likes to beat up smart
guys, yes?' he asks.

'Only when they don't spill the goods,' I snarl. 'Now cut the coming attractions and start counting the beans, before your jawbone does the man dance.'

The Prof stops and looks confused, then cackles and rushes back to his desk and starts scribbling notes on a pad.

'Fascinating language skills,' he mutters to himself. 'Ze subject talks almost total gibberish and yet I understand him completely.' He turns back to me. 'Would you, er, like ein apple strudel?'

'Save the hospitality, wise guy.' I'm in no mood for side projects. 'Just cut to the chase and we'll be out of your hair. Kieran—just the facts.'

'You vould like me to tell you about Kieran, yes?'

'As long as the day is dusty, then why not?' He stares at me with fascinated bemusement and I take the advantage and pour myself a quick drink of rye. 'How long have you known the target?'

'Oh, such a long time, mein liege,' he nods. 'He gave me ze brains to have ze brains, if you know vot I mean. Is funny, yes?'

'Like a cancer,' I mutter. 'I got some dealing to do and you might be able to help out. We need swift passage over to his compound and you're the kind of man who can handle his business. You tell us how to get there and we'll see your palms are greased with the finest green.'

'Fascinating, fascinating,' says the Prof, and walks close. 'And you are speaking English, yes?'

'The last time I checked.'

'I vould like to study you further, please,' says the Prof enthusiastically.

'No dice, Prof,' I tell him. 'No room for passengers where we're going.' But I look at Sue and she's giving me signals like we should take him along. I turn back to him. 'But on the other hand, let's see what you can offer.'

'Oh yes, I can offer goot stuff,' says the Prof, excited. 'I will need my larger brain for zis!'

And he runs off into the back of the lab and unscrews the top of his head, from the eyebrows up. He plucks out his brain, gets one the size of a small German shepherd, and then slams it in, screwing down a bigger forehead. 'Now ve are ready.'

SIXTY EIGHT

The Prof is in the back of the shark dressed in a trench coat, with a trilby perched on the top of his ridiculously large head. He smokes a pipe and mutters occasionally.

'Ze Kieran man iz a strange creature of many substanzes,' says the Prof, jabbing the pipe at me as we tear down the road. 'He has no perceptible blind spotz undt no obvious weaknesses. He is ... impenetrable.'

'You're talking crazy, Prof,' I tell him. 'Every man has a weakness.'

'Zis man iz a shard of steel in a large factory of impenetrable objects,' the Prof tells me. 'I haf known him for many years now undt haf seen nothing get ze better of him.'

'Yeah, but he hasn't met Joe Fury yet,' I say, and turn to face the way ahead just in time to see a puppy in the middle of the road. I slam on the brakes and the shark squeals to a halt, the front bumper inches from the puppy's head.

It yips.

'Could be a set-up,' I warn the others. 'Sit tight and wait for my all-clear.'

'I like zis man,' the Prof says to Sue. 'He is talking such utter nonsense.'

I slide out of the car with the cannon drawn. You can't expect anything too easy on a ride like this, and the closer we get to Kieran the more elaborate his traps become.

I give the dog the once over. It's small, brown and furry.

The dog yips at me and turns it's baby browns up. I level the popgun at it.

The Prof steps out of the car and laughs.

'I zink you haf become so agitated by zis job you haf taken zat you are seeing all kinds of bad zings where zere is nothing.' He bends down and picks up the puppy. 'See, it iz chust a puppy with cute eyes und a fluffy tail. Say "hello", Rover.'

'Hello,' says Rover.

SIXTY NINE

The Prof cuddles the animal. 'A talking dog. May my hairy gooseberries always deliver ze goods!'

'This isn't the dog talking, you moron,' says the voice. It's coming from a small speaker on the dog's neck. 'This is Kieran. God, no wonder I sacked you.'

'You didn't sack me!' the Prof rages at the sky. 'I quit. You are nuzzink but a cheapskate with a tiny vinky!'

'Flying sheep—what an idiot,' comes the voice of Kieran. 'Anyway, that's not important. I have the knowledge to destroy myself. This knowledge is contained in a small room on the edge of this road a hundred miles distant. If you want to end this game then find the knowledge and discover how to eliminate me. It's your choice.'

'Zuch a blow-hard,' mutters the Prof. 'I'm keeping ze dog as vell.'

It doesn't take us long to reach the room. It's got arrows painted all over the side of the building and hoardings screaming about 'The Knowledge.'

I skid the car to a halt and walk over to the door. I push it but it doesn't give. This is no time for subtlety so I step back and kick the door inwards.

And it's totally empty. Just a blank room.

The Prof turns up behind me with the dog, which starts to struggle in his arms.

'This some kind of metaphysical joke?' I ask the Prof. 'Because it if is, I'm going to kick his ass even harder than I intended to.'

'No. Votch.' He lets the dog go and it leaps into the room and vanishes.

Sue walks over and leans up against the threshold.

'It's cryptic, but then so is everything else on this road,' she says. 'You want to take a leap?'

'Anything you can add to this, Prof?' I ask.

'Yes,' he nods. 'I zink ve are ein shaften trousered.'

SEVENTY

'In all mein travels I have never encountered such a zing as zis.' The Prof is peering into the empty room. 'I have never developed anyzing like it, either. Flying sheep are easy—zis is something much more complicated.'

The Prof pokes an arm into the room. It doesn't disappear.

'I haf heard about zis place, and it has nuzzink to do vith Kieran. I zink he is tellink you vot is known as "za big bag of old badger's bollocks".'

The Prof turns to us.

'It is "Za Zone." You enter zis and all your dreams und fantasies vill be rewarded. Go on, Mr Fury, vot is your dream?'

'I don't have dreams. I just want to take down Kieran and get back to my whisky.'

'Zen it shall happen.'

I take a few steps towards the room, then hesitate.

'You first, Prof.'

'Votever you say.' And he steps into the zone and disappears. I snatch a glance at Sue, who shrugs.

'It's not my bag, honey,' she mutters, and I unholster the popgun, steady myself, and leap into the abyss.

SEVENTY ONE

The cage is locked from the outside and the Prof is laughing at me.

'You are zuch ein fool,' he witters, and wanders off into the darkness. I glance around but there's nothing to see except three walls of pipes and steel and an endless darkness ahead of the cage.

A second later Sue joins me.

'We got the quick trip up the creek, sister,' I mutter.

'Never trust a mad Professor.'

'We'll deal with him later,' I say, eyeing the shadows around us. 'First of all we need a one way ticket out of here.'

Sue tests the bars of the cage with a few yanks. 'Solid.'

'But that isn't.' I point upwards. The cage is suspended on a pulley system, with the bar it's hanging on leading off into the darkness.

'You sure this is a good idea?' asks Sue.

'We don't have a choice.' I slam myself against the cage and it shifts forwards an inch.

'This is too easy,' says Sue. 'Why set us up in this trap if it's so easy to move?'

'I've stopped worrying about questions like that, toots,' I tell her. 'Everything about this case seems like some kind of bad dream. But I've got a job to do.' I slam against the cage and it shifts forwards again. 'Besides, I've got to get back to the diner. I've got a clue about Kieran to pick up there.' I hand her the half note that the butler gave me and slam myself into the cage again.

This time it shifts further. The bar looks like it slopes downwards. This could be a bumpy ride.

'"Look".' Sue turns to me. 'What the hell does that mean?'

'Hang on, sister.' I slam the cage again. It tilts forwards and then starts to shift, gathering pace. 'This could be tight.'

Around us shadows flash past, looking like shapes in the gloom. Features. Faces. Arms. Claws. Eyes. All around us. As the cage picks up speed the pulley on the bar starts to shriek, metal grinding against steel.

'I think I see the end coming.' Sue points and there's definitely a wall in front of us, and it's approaching fast.

'Not even time for a Havana,' I mutter, and move to the back of the cage. Sue gets close and the wall gets closer.

SEVENTY TWO

We hit the wall like a rocket and smash through into the light. A short fall and we crash into the ground. The cage buckles and the door pops open.

I'm out like a flash and the gun is drawn. The place is white and quiet. Sue is out beside me with the Uzi in her hand.

'Analysis?' I ask her.

'Some kind of empty room,' she says. 'I suggest further investigation.'

'Sounds like a deal to me.'

We don't get time. A door in the far wall opens and a man in a kaftan and coloured glasses enters, a huge joint in his hand.

'Wow, daddio, and all that groovy kind of thing,' he croaks. 'Totally fantastic to see you, man. Like, drop in for a visit, why don't you?'

'You wanna try that in English?' I snap. 'I don't talk freak.'

'Heavy gig, man,' says the hippy. 'Like, chill. We always like a new face around this pad, man.'

'Where are we?' asks Sue. 'Er . . . man.'

'You're here, babe, right where you're standing.' The hippy

chokes on a lungful of smoke and hammers himself in the chest for what seems like a small age. 'Come on through and meet the gang.'

He beckons us and disappears through the doorway. There's nowhere to go but forwards, so we follow him.

The next room is a psychedelic blast of sheer insanity. The walls are a swirl of colours and paint spatters, like some insane Pollock has gone a step too far. Every square inch of the floor is covered in throw rugs and beanbags and every one has a hippy on it. The air is acrid with the stench of dope.

'What are your names, cats?' splutters the hippy.

'I'll ask the questions,' I tell him. Something isn't right about this set-up. How could so many hippies co-exist in one environment with so much dope. After all, someone has to order the pizzas. 'Who runs this joint?'

'You want a joint, man?' croaks a voice from the crowd. 'We got tonnes.'

'We all run it, man,' says the hippy. 'We're an autonomous collective. We, like, exist purely as a whole unit. All our problems are ... well, we don't have problems, man, because we're so stoned all the time.'

'Cooking, cleaning—all that kind of thing. Who does it?' This whole charade is starting to smell like last night's headlines.

'Oh, right, I get it.' The hippy starts nodding his head vigorously. He chokes down another monster sized toke of his joint and then coughs out a plume of smoke. 'The directors.'

'What, like company directors?'

'No way, man. Don't get heavy.' The hippy waves away the cloud of smoke and walks over to the end of the room. 'Take a look, man.' He pushes open a door.

The room is full of fat, bearded people in glasses, every one of them arguing.

'Goddammit, Coppola, it's a Pepperoni you asshole,' yells a small, bespectacled bearded man.

'Screw you, Spielberg! I'm the pizza king here, asshole!' screams a hairy fat guy.

'Film directors, man,' smiles the hippy. 'Like, we figured they all liked taking charge of things so much they could take over that kind of thing here.' He spares the sparring room a quick glance. 'Only problem is we can't get them to stop arguing, so not much ends up getting done.'

'Bummer,' says Sue.

'Total bummer. It's making me tense to the max, daddio,' chuckles the hippy, and then racks on another puff of the devil weed. 'Or it would be if I wasn't smoking this.' And he is overcome by fits of giggles that send him collapsing to the floor.

I grab Sue by the hand. 'Come on. There's gotta be a way out of here.'

There is. The floor opens up beneath us.

SEVENTY THREE

We crash through the ceiling of the diner where we met Preston and land in a tangled heap. Sue doesn't look worried.

'Fury, you did it!' shouts Preston, and starts towards us with his popgun drawn. I reach for mine and he aims for my least vulnerable part. 'Stow it, Fury,' he snaps, all smiles gone. 'I don't care if it's on purpose or by mistake. The woman's mine. Now back off slowly and I won't feel the need to fill you full of lead.'

I back up, hands raised. 'Can I smoke?'

'You can do whatever feels necessary,' says Preston. 'Just keep your hands off the gun.'

I snap out a Havana and spark a match. 'Looks like the journey's over, honey. It's been a ride.'

Sue's on her feet and in Preston's grasp quick-time. She looks back at me, concerned. 'Say it ain't so, Joe.'

'The game's up.' I take a puff on the cigar. 'I'd like to help you out, but the man has a gun on me.'

'That's right, Joe.' Preston edges the barrel towards me. 'One false move and I'll put a hole in you.'

'Take the girl, Preston,' I say, with a dismissive wave of my hand. 'Just one thing. Why do you want her back so badly?'

'She's the key to Kieran,' he says, and there's a gleam in his eye that's full of insane glory.

'There's a lot of keys to Kieran,' I mutter. 'He's got more holes than Bonnie and Clyde.'

'It was nice knowing you, Joe,' nods Preston with a smile.

'But this is one private dick who doesn't close his case.' And he aims the gun at me.

Sue sparks into action. Well, she tries to, but Preston's too quick. Before she can stamp on his foot and turn his gonads into puree with her fingernails he twists her arm up behind her and wrenches it hard. And she's down on her knees.

'I'm no mug, Suzanne,' he says, leaning close to her, and I see my chance. I finger the Havana and zero in on a spot on his hand. Burning tip. Human flesh. Not a good combination. And I've got just one chance.

'Get off my back,' shouts Sue, and the wall behind them explodes.

SEVENTY FOUR

It's Professor Spanner, and he's riding the weirdest machine I've ever seen. It's about the size of a small truck, with all kinds of death dealers sprouting from the front—knives, rotary saws, flame-throwers.

The Prof doesn't look happy. His eyes are gleaming with hatred and anger. And he's staring straight at me.

'You doggen shaggen!' he screams at me. 'You let my hippies out!'

Sue wrenches herself out of Preston's stunned grip and they split, Sue going one way and Preston the other as the death machine crashes through the diner towards us.

'I didn't touch your hippies, Prof,' I say, whipping out the popgun and nailing a buzzing rotary saw.

'They jumped through zer hole in der floor, you dumbkopf!' he screams, gunning the engine.

'Drop the accent, Prof,' I shout. 'You're a fraud.' And I aim with a squint and fire clear and true. The bullet snatches off the Prof's face at the ear. Underneath there's nothing but a ninja mask.

The machine lurches forward and suddenly I'm up against the wall, the saws inches from my face.

'No one dares unmask the Naked Avenger!' booms the voice from the mask, and he suddenly jerks and slumps forwards over the controls of the machine, revealing one of the hippies behind him with a huge syringe.

'Man, what a dose,' chuckles the hippy.

'Nice work, freak,' I say, and swing the cannon around to aim for Preston. But it's too late. He disappears out over the rubble and he's nothing but a memory.

The hippy jumps down from the machine and offers me a doobie. I decline.

'Nice job, man,' he says through the smoke. 'We were, like, wandering around because the door was wide open and then saw this, like, groovy hole in the floor, so we took the ultimate trip, man.' He looks around. 'Where are we?'

'Right where I need you.'

'Get that machine out of there!' yells a voice, and I look across to see one of the fat, beardy directors stalking around like a mini-dictator. 'I will have no death-dealing devices on my goddamn set!'

'Can it, short stuff,' I growl, and the director runs off to a corner to hide. I turn to the hippy. 'You're gonna have a lot of trouble with those guys around.'

'Hey, we need them, man.' The hippy smiles. 'Scorsese! I, like, could do with a pizza, man.'

One of the directors nods and rushes off to the phone.

'How'd you get that kind of control?' I ask.

The hippy holds up a small bag of white powder. 'Keeps them happy.'

I make my farewells and clamber over the rubble to where Sue's standing.

'Looks like I missed out on the second half of the message.' I tell her.

'Are you sure about that?' she says, and points off into the distance.

Out there, carved on the side of a distant mountain, is the word 'OUT.'

Sue unravels the other half of the message and holds it up for me to see. 'Remember the first part?'

'Damn.' The whole note reads 'LOOK OUT.'

That's when the H-bomb hits. Right on top of us.

SEVENTY FIVE

A large white sphere surrounds us in an instant, and we're sitting in padded chairs gazing at the raging fire that curls in slow motion around us.

The opposite half of the sphere is in darkness, and there's something moving in it. I can guess who. 'Kieran,' I say.

'Yes.' The tone is low and indistinct, sounding like it's made up of many voices.

'What party trick are you pulling now?'

'It's not a trick,' says the darkness that is Kieran. No features, just a vague form. 'Just an example.'

'Of what,' I snap, 'how much of a cheap magician you are?'

'This isn't hypnosis or illusion,' replies Kieran. 'It's a warning. Just an example of the power I can wield. Just an example of what I can do. To you.'

'Nice try, smart guy,' I tell him. 'Give up the charade and introduce yourself like a man.'

The shadow shifts imperceptibly. 'I am much more than a man, Mr Fury. I am the way forward for all humanity. I am the all-seeing eye and the spider in the web.'

'What is this? Improv theatre?' I take out a cigar and spark the end. 'What's stopping me pulling out the popgun and plugging you right here, Einstein?'

'Everything.' And the raging fireball around us suddenly retracts, sucked into the depths of the shadow's hands until it's nothing but a pinprick of light. Kieran closes his palms and it disappears. 'I have the power of destruction. I am the end of all things. I am what's—'

'Yeah, yeah.' I wave him away through a cloud of smoke. 'You're also a first class bore. I've got a cannon in my pocket that says this game is over. Now come quietly like a good stooge and maybe I won't have to get rough.'

'You don't seem to understand the situation you are in, Mr Fury. You are playing with the very forces of nature, and you will lose.'

'And you're playing with the forces of cliché, wise guy.' But I keep the popgun in my jacket. Something tells me this isn't the right time to push it. 'What's with the ninja disguised as the Prof? You can't do the dirty work yourself?'

'The ninja is not my doing,' says the shadow that is Kieran. 'There are more forces after the girl than you can possibly imagine.'

'Okay, end of discussion.' I get up off the chair and start towards the shadow. 'Time to say hello to papa.'

But the white sphere disappears, and so does the shadow that's Kieran. I turn to Sue. 'What the hell was that all about?'

'He's playing with you,' says Sue. 'It's his stock in trade. He'll screw around with your mind and reel you in like a fish. Before you know it you'll be putty in his hands. He's just softening you up for the kill.'

'The man's a grade "A" moron,' I say, and then notice the phalanx of ninjas behind Sue, all with their katanas out. It's not a pretty sight. 'Head up, toots,' I say, pulling out the gun. 'Looks like we've got trouble.'

SEVENTY SIX

'Jesus, almost wasted a good stoogie,' I say, as I finish off the Havana. We're sitting atop a pile of unconscious ninjas. It's surprising what a good pair of fists and a bit of moxy can do. 'Where did he drag these idiots up from?'

'I think it's the nuns,' says Sue.

'Nuns or no nuns, we're taking that sucker in.' I stub the cigar out on a ninja and climb down the pile to the shark. 'Coming?'

'It's the only way to travel.' Sue climbs down and joins me in the front of the car. One stomp on the gas later we're streaming forwards to our destiny. I only hope they serve a good shot of whisky at the end of it.

SEVENTY SEVEN

You don't expect to see a huge towering gothic castle in the middle of the desert. Especially not one with a 'Welcome' sign outside of it. But these days I'd gotten used to that kind of thing.

'I'm feeling peckish, toots. Fancy a bite?'

Sue nods and we pull in to the front of the castle. I already know this is going to be trouble, but when a man has to eat nothing can get in his way. There's a fat, sweating man at the front door of the castle dressed in a loud suit and holding a microphone.

'Aye up, ladies and bastids!' he says. 'Looks like we got a couple of ripe ones here.' He holds out his hand as an introduction and we ignore it.

'Which way to the bar?' I ask.

'Aye, lad, my mother in law's so fat she's quite bloody big. Because she eats tons of food. And she likes chocolate a lot.' The fat man looks confused for a second.

'You should be on stage,' I mutter, and we enter the castle.

'My mother in law's so fat,' says the fat man, 'she should probably be a comedian.'

We make our way through cobwebbed halls towards the sound of a small crowd. A door with a sign saying 'Free Entry and Food' leads the way into a vast, cavernous night-club.

The patrons are scattered listlessly around the room. They all look hollow-eyed and brain-dead. At the front of the room, on the stage, a man in a glittery tux and glasses is going through the usual.

'Eh, politicians, eh?' says the comedian. 'Can't trust them, can you? They all lie. But then you know that anyway. So it's not funny.' He taps the mic. 'I know this thing's on, I'm just trying to get a cheap laugh out of the fact that I'm so crap.'

'I hope they're not paying this guy.' I say, and hit the bar.

It's long, sleek, and black as midnight. The barman glides up. He's wearing a cape and it's hard not to stare at his fangs.

'What can I get you?' he hisses. 'Bloody Mary? A Screaming Bloody Death? A Cup Full of Blood? Or a mojito?'

'Two mojitos,' I tell him. 'Got any food?'

'Oh, plenty,' he says, and glances towards the stage. He slopes off wringing his hands and chuckling to himself.

'Get me some steaks?' I yell after him, and he freezes for a second before turning to face me with a leer.

'Would you like them raw or ... ' A pause. 'Or, er, not raw?'

'Well done—two of them.' I turn and face the stage as the comedian walks off to no applause. He's replaced by another middle aged man in a shiny suit who starts banging out a witless song on an out-of-tune piano.

'I'm getting a good idea what's in store for us here,' says Sue, and she checks the Uzi. 'Locked and loaded.'

The bartender slopes back, chucking the drinks down in front of us.

'What's the damage?' I ask.

'Your personality!' he hisses. Sue jams the Uzi into his face and he shuts up quick and sharp.

'Take me to your leader, asshole,' she says, and the barman nods and scuttles off. We follow.

The room he leads us to is full of priceless ornaments and furniture, all centred around a man the size of a small orbiting planet who's spread out on a huge bed. His stomach spills over the sides.

'Come in, my friends,' bloats the man, wiggling his sausage-like fingers at a couch. 'Take the weight off your mucklucks.'

'We're just looking for food,' I say. 'It doesn't take a genius to figure out what kind of set up you got here. Bad comedians. Bad singers. Bad vibes. You rip the talent out of people and suck it in for yourself, right?'

'Ah,' says the man. 'You have an uncanny gift for spotting the obvious.'

'I also have a gift for putting your nose out of joint with this,' I say, whipping out the cannon. 'Just feed us the meat, fats, and cut the melodrama.'

The man looks shocked and his face falls. 'You disappoint me. I could have done with some proper entertainment. The acts we book these days are so limp and lifeless. We need fresh *meat, dammit!*' He tries to rise out of the bed, but just writhes around like a beached whale for a few seconds.

'Try a proper promoter,' I say. 'Now, we need something with substance, so cough up the goods.'

'Such a disappointment,' the man mutters again, and his stomach buckles and bulges, then unzips down the front, revealing a spindly mullet-haired man inside. 'Let's go to the dining room.'

SEVENTY EIGHT

It's well laid out and we tear through the steaks like they're going out of fashion.

'Nice work,' I say to the man, as he picks at a salad. 'Now what's going on in this joint? Last I heard vampires fed off blood.'

'We're not vampires,' says the man. 'Well, not technically. Just a troupe of out of work actors, comedians and travelling toilet salesmen who wanted to set up a place we could call our home. The fact that we happen to suck the talent out of people is just one of those things. In reality we're fakes. Look.' He raps on the wall. It sounds like cardboard. 'Even the building's a fake.'

'Why go to all this trouble?' asks Sue as she wipes juice off her lip.

'Because we have no choice,' says the man. 'My name's Reginald. I'm a stand-up comedian by trade, and a magician by choice.' He snaps out a stuffed dove from his pocket and beats it on the table for good measure.

No one laughs.

'See, we're doomed.' He hangs his head. 'We're trying to find the essence of entertainment. What truly makes someone funny, or talented, or—as one of my esteemed colleagues once put it—"not shit".'

'Try hard work and a sense of humour,' I tell him, and stand up. 'We've got places to go and people to deal with, so we'll take a hike.'

'We need your help, Fury,' pleads the man. 'Your reputation travels far and wide. We need to find out what's blocking us from sucking the best bits of talent out of the people who come here. We can help you. We know you're on a quest to take down Kieran.'

'Don't tell me he set you up in this gin joint,' I mutter.

'No, not a bit of it.' The man shakes his head. 'We did play a few nights for him once, but he robbed us of everything we deemed worthy.'

'Your money?' offers Sue.

'Worse,' replies the man. 'Our cocks.'

'I don't take charity cases,' I tell him.

'If you help us, I can offer you some important information about Kieran.'

'I've got more info than I could fill a Mac truck with.' I start towards the door. 'Sayonara.'

'We've also got money!'

'Make me an offer.' I stop and face him.

'There's a vortex in the basement of this building, and it's feeding off the talent that stops by. It's taking away from us what we need. What we came here for in the first place. And we need it stopped. Plugged up. Do this for us and we will reward you with more riches than you can possibly want.'

'Come on, toots.' I nod to Sue. 'Let's blow this pop stand.'

She looks at me. Her eyes tell me she's intrigued. My pop-gun tells me I should plug this joker and head for the hills. But I give in, resigned.

'Okay, short stuff,' I say to the man, with a sigh. 'Point us in the right direction.'

He does. It's an endless vortex full of the screaming souls of the damned.

'A walk in the park,' I mutter. Then the vortex leaps forward and closes around us, and we're dragged into the eternity of damnation.

SEVENTY NINE

It's time for the popgun to make an entrance. A screaming soul races right for us and Sue whips up the Uzi and lays a ream of fire towards it. But the bullets punch misty holes through the soul and it keeps on coming.

I swing a fist and it crashes through its jaw. The soul passes straight through me and for a split second the life of the damned fills my head. And it's dull. Instead of torment and pain, it's recipes for rice cakes and tips on knitting.

I see a soul whip through Sue and she stares at me in stunned horror. 'It's so ... so boring!' she says in surprise.

'That's eternal damnation for you, honey.' Ahead of us there's a thousand million screaming souls all waiting for a taste of us. 'We could use some of Chicago's influence with this baby.'

I decide to take a direct approach. 'What kind of wiseguy put you in this place?' I yell at the damned, but get nothing but confused looks back. Great, they're dumb as well as boring.

'This really is damnation,' mutters Sue.

'Don't knock it, toots. At least it's better than TV.'

Just then a pimped up flying milk float screeches to a stop next to us. It's piloted by a man with a bad suit and a smile as false as his hair.

'Hop in, Fury,' says the man. 'It's time to take the short cut.'

EIGHTY

We don't need telling twice. We're up and in the milk float and the toupee man kicks the vehicle into gear and we're off. The damned souls behind us just look confused.

'What's with all the farmed souls?' I ask him.

' "Farmed souls" are exactly the right words, Mr Fury,' says the man, as we fly through a slit of light in the vortex, and out into a vast chamber stretching off into the distance.

Below us lie row after row of huge generators. Workmen in goggles, suits and gloves cram confused looking souls into the machines, which whirr and grind steel against steel, before small blue glowing lights pop out into huge metal bins.

'I'm the Farmer,' says the man. 'It's a bit of a complex operation, but basically we're farming the souls for ideas.'

'Business looks like it's booming,' I say, sparking up another cigar.

'The problem is those bloody vampire entertainers keep blocking up the entrance,' says the Farmer. 'Now we've got a backlog as big as the moon.'

'Just take out the vampires,' I tell him. 'Simple as!'

'Unless you haven't noticed, we don't really exist in the corporeal world,' explains the Farmer. 'We're living on the edge of existence—literally. Dreams, nightmares, the whole kit and caboodle. We're responsible for those. We take the ideas from the souls.'

'What do you do with the ideas?' asks Sue.

'We feed them back into the world,' explains the Farmer. 'That's why the same ideas keep cropping up century after century. There's nothing new out there, but if it wasn't for us regurgitating the ideas back out, there would literally be nothing. No entertainment, no books, no films, nothing. And now these vampire jokers are stopping the flow. They suck the souls, leaving us with nothing but what you experienced—knitting patterns and blandness—for those that manage to squeeze in. It's hopeless.'

'Well, that explains their stage show.' Sue glances around. 'But their castle isn't the only source of talent in the world. You've got an entire planet to take it from.'

'They've stuck their castle right over our conduit.' The Farmer sighs. 'We can't get out there and take down their operation, because we can't exist in their world. But you can.'

'What's in it for us?' Another bargain on the flip side of reality. I'm getting used to these.

The Farmer squares me with a solid look. 'You want to find a quick way into the heart of Kieran?'

'Surprise me.'

And he does.

EIGHTY ONE

It's sitting on a pedestal. And it's a key. 'This will get you into the storm drains of Kieran's compound,' says the Farmer. 'No messing about. Just pop it in and Bob's your Fanny's auntie.'

'You got a deal,' I tell him.

I pluck the key off the pedestal and the Farmer kicks the milk float into a spin and takes us back to the slit in the vortex.

'Good luck, Mr Fury.' The Farmer waves us off with a smile. 'Whether you know it or not, there's a lot of vested interest in you taking down Kieran.'

'I'm starting to get that impression,' I mutter, and seconds later we're back in the room with the empty, deflated body of the fat man. The small guy inside of him looks surprised.

'Er, lovely,' he says, confused. 'Have any trouble?'

'Just you,' I tell him, and spark a match to re-light my Havana. The man's eyes widen as he realises what I'm doing.

'We had a deal!' he shrieks, but the match is flying. It hits the shabby wall and the place goes up like a tinderbox. *'Attack!'* he yells, and comes for me with his teeth out. His fingers stretch and the nails shoot out until they're about a foot long. His face warps into ragged skin and blazing red eyes.

I'm taking out the popgun, but Sue's there and rakes a blast across him. It knocks him down, but not out.

'Let's boost!' I turn and head for the door, but there's a

hissing, screaming mass of nails and eyes in front of us. Sue blows a hole through the first layer and I wade in with my fists, punching through the head of something big and ugly, with fangs as long as my arms.

'Let's face it,' screams Sue as she takes out the nads of the nearest vampire. 'This isn't the worst we've been in.'

But we're locked in by the writhing mass of fury that's coming towards us. One vampire clamps a claw into my coat and I throw it over my shoulder, then stamp on its head. The skull explodes into a liquid mess.

'This way!' Sue points to a flight of stairs and we're up, laying down line after line of gunfire as the vampires crawl at us from below and above.

Something big is ahead of us. It's all spiky limbs and angular bones. Shoulders crunch against the ceiling as it swings a faceful of gleaming teeth at us and swipes.

I duck and it almost takes me out. Sue hammers a burst into its teeth and it howls and screams and comes for us quick and fast.

I grab Sue round the waist and leap off the staircase, sailing over the grasping arms before I catch onto the chandelier with my gun hand. Sue hammers shots into the faces below, tearing out eyes and teeth and bone, and splashing blood and bad jokes in all directions.

We swing long as the fire spreads up the staircase, and the momentum carries us sailing over the vampires and straight for the front door. We land on our feet and make a break for the shark as the comedian vampire at the entrance looks on confused, mid-routine.

I'm behind the wheel, gunning the engine, and we screech off down the road, leaving the howling mob behind us. But it's not as easy as I first thought. The castle might be burning and their numbers might be depleted, but I never figured they could raise a convoy.

EIGHTY TWO

They've got trucks decked out with spikes and cars chopped and cut and boosted with huge engines belching smoke and pain.

'I'll choose the restaurant next time,' yells Sue against the wind, and she sends a hurl of bullets into the nearest car, taking out the tyres. They burst and the car tips and stumbles and goes over on its side, rolling end over end before a huge, monstrous truck punches it out of the way. Eyes and teeth are behind the wheel, but it's no match for my cannon.

I aim sweet and sure down the barrel and punch off a shot. It separates the eyes and the head explodes into a bloody mess.

The truck starts to list, the front end spinning wide. The rear end jack-knifes and the truck keels over like a dying animal, taking out a few of the pursuing vehicles. But there's plenty left.

'I've got an idea,' I shout, and stamp on the brake.

Sue almost goes over the bonnet, but the shark sails back into the convoy and they part like the Red Sea.

It's confusion. Cars slam into each other and huge battle wagons collide and wrench steel from steel. A car to our left explodes as it rams into the back of another vehicle. Screaming vampires spill off in all directions.

They make easy targets.

One hand on the wheel, I start spinning left, right, and centre, taking out heads and limbs. Bullets slam into engine blocks and gas tanks and vehicles blossom into fire and spare parts.

Sue gets the idea and starts raking the Uzi in all directions, carving bodies in half and sending the pack into bloody, panicked confusion.

Except for the fifty foot battle wagon behind us. It's as tall as it is long, bristling with weapons of every description, and it crashes through the mania with no concern for anyone.

'Take the wheel!' I scream at Sue, and she grabs it and guns the engine. We fishtail off as the bullets start to rake the air around us, punching holes in the shark. It's time for some extreme action.

I climb onto the back of the shark and leap for the battle wagon.

EIGHTY THREE

They've got so much armour and weaponry that landing safely is a piece of cake. A machine gun swings towards me and I pop a cap in the vampire's head. The gun swings down, taking out the gun emplacement below.

I crawl upwards with the wind tearing at me, up onto the roof of the vehicle. All guns swing in my direction. I eat the roof as bullets start flying, taking out more of their own kind, then I swing the cannon around, popping heads off like it's a duck shoot. Easy pickings.

When the roof's clear, I lower myself on to the sloping side of the battle wagon and spot my way in: a bolt hole with a rifle sticking out of it.

I grab the rifle and pull, and a vampire comes sailing out looking nonplussed. He gets a moment to register the fact that he's hit the road before a car runs over him.

I'm through the bolt hole and firing away. The first shot ricochets and takes out a row of vampires who are caught unawares, but that's my only surprise and I'm running for the door at the far end of the corridor.

The jackpot. A ladder leading down to the sound of the screaming engine.

I drop down and come face to face with a confused looking engineer. I flick him away with a wave of the cannon and he backs off. I make for the gas tanks at the rear of the truck.

Suddenly the engineer vampire comes at me with teeth bared, and knocks me down. I get a foot on his neck and push, but it's like he's made of elastic and the head strains down towards me while the neck stretches back.

I headbutt the arrogance out of him and he goes down squealing like a pig, clutching his teeth. I get up, grab an axe, and put a big, ugly hole in the gas tank. If I can't destroy it then I can knock it out of action.

Then fortune smiles on me. There's a wooden chair by the machinery, and I pick it up and shatter it, then rip the shirt off the screaming vampire and soak it in gasoline. Sparking up a Havana with the flick of a match, I set the shirt alight. A sack of grenades would have been better, but chances like this don't come every Sunday.

I throw the burning shirt onto the wood as the gasoline seeps towards it. Then I'm up and out of the engine room as quick as my legs will carry me.

On the hallway deck the vampires are gathering, but I've got bullets left for all of them. They die easy and I'm out of the bolt hole and back up on the roof of the battle wagon. Sue sees me and cuts the engine back, raking the pursuing cars with Uzi fire as she slides alongside.

'I don't normally pick up hitch-hikers,' she shouts. But I'm not here for the comedy. I leap into the car and she guns the engine and we take off, screaming away from the battle wagon as it starts to slow.

We're a good distance away when the gas tank goes up. The explosion takes out the cars around it, sending burning vehicles all over the space, spinning through the air, leaving trails of fire and smoke. Engines detonate and there's panic and mayhem as cars with flaming gas tanks zigzag and go up in burning fireballs.

The pursuit tails off into smoke and confusion and we're away down the road, leaving it all behind us.

'Thanks for the help, honey,' I say, as I slide into the driving seat. That's when I feel the barrel of a gun against the back of my neck.

EIGHTY FOUR

I glance in the rear view mirror. Nixon sits on the back seat, along with Reagan, Lincoln and Kennedy.

'Ex-presidents,' I mutter. 'You're worse than cockroaches.'

'Cut the chatter and listen to me,' snaps Nixon, digging the piece into the back of my neck. 'We need safe passage out of here. We've been promised a resurgence in popularity, and Kieran's the only man who knows how to give it to us. Word on the street says you're the man who's going in that direction, so stay quiet and keep driving.'

'What's Kennedy doing here?' I ask.

'He makes us look good,' snaps Nixon.

'Hey, baby.' Kennedy shifts forward in the seat and nestles up to Sue. 'Fancy letting me park my missile in your Bay of Pigs?'

She slaps him around the face. 'Stow it, smoothie. I'm not in the mood for any of your crap. People tend to forget you almost kick-started a third world war.'

'Hell, I got some decent poontang out of it.' And Kennedy chuckles.

'Are we home yet?' Reagan whines. 'I want to play with my toys!'

'We're almost there, Reagan,' soothes Nixon. 'Just hang on until the end of the world.'

'What end of the world?' I lock eyes with Nixon in the rear view mirror. He knows he's said too much.

'Nothing, nothing.' Nixon shrinks back, shaking his head.

'Spill the beans,' I snap, and Nixon flinches. 'You're sweating like a pig in a slaughter house. What's the beef?'

'Jesus, not again,' sighs Kennedy. 'You're about as subtle as a kick in the nuts.' Kennedy leans forward and pushes Nixon back. With the gun off my neck I've got a better chance of taking out these goons. 'It's just a slip of the tongue. We just need to make the world a better place. A better place full of chicks with great hooters!'

'Can it, Kennedy.' I'm not in the mood for this crap. 'When Nixon slips it's the truth. What's the low-down on Armageddon?'

There's a lot of uncomfortable glances swapped between Kennedy and Nixon. Reagan plays with a button on his shirt, looking oblivious. Lincoln stares stoically off into the middle distance. It takes me a few seconds, but I catch on he's a stuffed dummy.

'What's with the stiff?' I ask.

'Dammit, Reagan, I told you this wouldn't work.' Nixon toys with the gun and gives Reagan a look that tells me he's not averse to putting a bullet in his head.

'I like fries in brown gravy!' splutters Reagan, and then carries on playing with his button.

'My friend, my friend,' says Kennedy, holding out his hands placatingly. 'It was all Reagan's idea. He thought it might add credibility to our campaign to bring peace to this great world of ours.'

'Cough up on the Armageddon theory, wise guy!'

'You seem to forget, I've got the weapon.' Nixon swings

the gun around towards us again. 'Now take us to Kieran or we'll see what the inside of your head looks like.'

Sue's not taking any more of this. She whips out the Uzi. Nixon aims the gun at her and I snap round and slap him smartly around the head. He cries like a baby and Sue snatches the gun out of his hand.

'We've got the advantage now, Nixon,' she says. 'Spill it.'

'It's Kieran,' sobs Nixon. 'It's all part of a conspiracy. He promised us what we all aimed for when we were in power. The end of the world.' He sits up and grasps the back of the seat, panicked. 'The conspiracy theories, Fury! They're all true!'

'Illuminati, Priory of Scion—all that kind of thing?' Just rumours and paranoia.

'All of it!' pleads Nixon. 'The FBI and the CIA showed us the dossier. The forces of evil will take over the world if we don't do something to stop it. And by dammit, we tried! You have no idea how difficult it is trying to kick-start the end of the world.'

Kennedy slaps him around the back of the head. 'Nice going, dickwad. Now that's the end of this little scam.'

'It's not a scam,' yells Nixon. 'It's the only way to save the world from itself. War, famine, death, destruction, genocide, peace—the world can't suffer any more of this misery!'

'No offence, Nixon, but you don't strike me as a pacifist.' I take my hands off the wheel and light a cheroot. 'There's more to this than meets the genocidal maniac. What's Kieran got to do with it?'

'Everything!' says Nixon. 'He's the man who can bring our dreams to triumph. He can destroy this world and rule over the other!'

'The other?' This case is getting more convoluted by the second.

'The other world!' yells Nixon, frothing at the mouth. 'The dark world!'

And suddenly we're sucked out of the shark and into a courtroom.

EIGHTY FIVE

It's wide and spacious and the public gallery is stuffed to the gills with men, women and those in between, of all creeds and colours.

At the front of the room, in the judge's chair, sits a chimp in an English barrister's wig, holding a gavel and staring down at us with malign intent. I blow smoke in his direction.

We're seated—all of us—in front of the judge. Nixon is wringing his hands, Reagan has a finger up his nose, and Kennedy's trying to chat up a female juror by unzipping his pants.

'You stand accused of crimes against being groovy!' booms the chimp judge. 'And for speaking out of the bounds of your contract with your lord and master. How do you plead?'

'I only did it for the good of the country!' cries Nixon, falling to his knees. 'Don't condemn me for my legitimate actions on the world stage.'

'You have condemned yourself,' booms the judge, hammering the gavel a few times for emphasis. 'Now you hold yourself open to trial by chimp. Kennedy, get your hands off of those.'

Kennedy smiles sheepishly and returns to his seat.

'Kennedy, I know you think you're the golden boy!' The chimp judge points the gavel at him. 'But the public forget what kind of person you really are. They forget the war you started and the people's blood on your hands. A nice smile and a charming personality are not enough to wipe away your dreams of Armageddon.'

The chimp judge turns on Nixon. 'You, on the other hand, have a soul as black as midnight. You hang a veil of compromise, negotiation and peace over your deeds, and yet you still manage to escalate what Kennedy started. You are filled with dreams of genocide and mass extermination, and blame everyone else but yourself.'

'And you are a *moron!*' Reagan doesn't even notice the chimp judge screaming at him. He goes on picking his nose. 'You were led by the nose with dreams of duplicity in Hollywood and dreams of extermination in your White House years, and normally you would suffer for your crimes. But I have a bargain in store for all three of you.'

The chimp judge hops down from behind the bench and waddles over. 'How would you turkeys like a third strike at the end of existence? I could use some people like you.'

Nixon nods like an excited dog, while Kennedy winks at the female jurors and nods towards his crotch.

The chimp judge turns on Sue. 'And as for you, Suzanne Bloch, it's time to meet the end of your life.'

The wall explodes and a brace of nuns run in.

EIGHTY SIX

I pull out the popgun and take the first one down. Sue grabs the chimp and holds him up by the throat, the Uzi aimed for his head.

It doesn't stop the nuns.

'You can't harm me!' screeches the chimp judge. 'I'm not even here.' And he pops out of existence.

The dead presidents head for the hole in the wall.

'Sayonara, baby,' laughs Nixon with a salute. 'See you on the flipside, flatfoot.' And he's through, with Kennedy and Reagan in tow. The bigger problem of more armed nuns heads in our direction.

'Back of the room!' I shout, but Sue's already there, laying down a stream of bullets to cover our tracks.

We burst out of the court and we're back in the desert, by the road, the shark idling nearby. Sue slams the door shut behind us and the whole building wobbles uncertainly and then crashes down, burying the nuns, who curse and swear and pray behind us.

'What a stroke of luck,' says Sue, then she turns and stops, staring over my shoulder. Her look says everything. We're in at the deep end without a paddle.

I turn to see a thousand ninjas lined up before us, all with weapons in their hands, all tense and ready to pounce.

'Brace yourself, sugar,' I say, getting between her and the ninjas. 'This could be the end of the road.'

The head ninja walks slowly forward and reaches into his tunic. I level the gun at him. So far there's no sign of attack, but the first one that makes any dangerous moves gets aerated.

Instead the ninja takes out a scroll and bows low, holding

it towards me. Keeping the popgun on him, I take the scroll and unroll it.

'You are cordially invited to take tea and whisky in the presence of Her Mother Superior at the Church of the Immaculate Immolation' it reads.

'Fancy a shot of the good stuff?' I offer Sue. 'Because we don't have a choice.'

EIGHTY SEVEN

The Mother Superior is built like a brick outhouse. She's got stubble on her chin, a face like a punch bag, and the robes that shroud her body can't hide a bulk the size of a small orbiting planet.

'Tea?' she grunts, and offers a tiny cup in her ape-like fist.

Sue shakes her head. 'Hit me with the hard stuff.' She nods to the whisky, and in no time we're knocking back the bourbon and eyeing up the exits.

'To what do we owe this pleasure?' I ask, trying to be cordial. The butt of the cannon pokes out of my jacket, and in a fair fight I could whip this penguin into shape. But when have nuns ever been fair?

The chief penguin turns her gaze on Sue. She's trying to look sympathetic but it's like watching a Republican trying to shake hands with a gay rights campaigner.

'Suzanne, my dear.' The Mother Superior smiles and a mirror across the room shatters. 'Such a disappointment. We only wanted you to enter the fold and embrace the harmony of our ways.'

'Kieran didn't give me up for that,' snaps Sue, and she gets out of the chair and approaches the nun. The Mother Superior recoils into her chair. 'He gave me up because of what I know and what I wouldn't do. You know that.'

'All I know is a world of peace and harmony and serving our dear Lod—er, Lord.' The Mother Superior smiles sheepishly. 'You had the option of leaving once your time here had been served.'

Sue points a finger at a clock on the wall. The hands don't move. 'You know very well we're trapped in time, so don't feed me that line. Time in this dump means time in eternity.'

'You're back now,' says the penguin. 'Back into the fold. If you would just join us we can learn to live in harmony with one another.'

'Is that why you got the ninjas?' I say. The Mother Superior shifts her gaze to me. 'Nuns with guns not got the shakes to bring in one detective and a woman?'

'The ninjas were a necessary evil,' says the nun, trying to be graceful. 'Our field operatives have proven to be less than effective.'

The Mother Superior gets up and the building shifts under her weight.

'You're free to go, Mr Fury. You were never part of the bargain. All we wanted was the girl. All we wanted was to return her to the bosom of Grod—er, God. Surely you can understand that?'

'What's in it for me?'

'The road to Kieran.' The Mother Superior points out of the window. In the distance stands a tall tower. 'That is where he lies. That is where he lives. The girl has been returned to us. I have an express car waiting outside for you right now.'

'And what if I don't?'

'We have the ninjas to help us.'

'And all I've got to do is hand over the moll?'

The Mother Superior smiles at me. 'Precisely.'

'Why's she so precious to you?'

'She has certain . . . assets we need to take advantage of.'

I glance at Sue and she drops her eyes. 'I can tell what kind of assets she's got, sister.' I turn to the Mother Superior. 'As far as I can tell the moll's used up all her favours with me. You can take her, do what you want. I've got a case to get on with and I can't spare the time for negotiating with penguins. Expect a bill from me.'

It takes a second for the pun to sink in, but when it does the nun chuckles like crunching gravel.

'Very clever, Mr Fury. Now if you'll go downstairs, my driver will take you directly to Kieran.'

I nod and walk towards the door. Then pause.

'Just one thing?' I turn to face the nun. She waits expectantly. 'What happens when an unstoppable action meets an unmoveable force?'

The nun looks confused for a second. 'I've no idea.'

'Joe Fury kicks both their asses.' And I sock the Mother Superior in the jaw and send her flying. That's when all hell breaks loose.

EIGHTY EIGHT

The door pops open and two ninjas leap through, but their cold steel is no match for my popgun, which plugs them both square in the forehead.

Sue's beside me as we crash through the door, taking out a handful of nuns who are cleaning a heavy machine gun that's aimed straight at the threshold.

'Lot of firepower,' I mutter, as I take down a screaming ninja who's flying through the air towards us. 'You must carry some heavy baggage.'

'You can't imagine,' says Sue, kicking the teeth out of a ninja who's trying to sneak up behind her.

'Care to tell me the story?' I smack a nun in the jaw, then ventilate a couple of fat comedy ninjas who are trying to attack us with strings of sausages.

'It's like I told you before,' says Sue, elbowing a nun in the ribs and then slapping her a few times around the face, before drop kicking her through the window. 'I was Kieran's piece, his moll, his floozy. He used me and when I couldn't offer him any more loving he tried to put me away, so my knowledge about his compound could never get out.'

'You didn't say that before.' I grab a nun around the head and run her straight into a wall. 'Your story keeps changing, sister. Now speak up.'

'You don't understand, Fury,' says Sue, straight arming a ninja in the nuts and then finishing him off with a roundhouse kick. 'There's never a single strand with Kieran. Every story has a thousand variations depending on what he feeds into your mind. He really is the king of reality.'

'Reality, my grandmother's balls,' I snap, popping several caps into a group of nuns who are raging towards us with blazing machine guns. 'This is just more veiled stories. There has to be a truth somewhere.'

'That's exactly the point.' Sue bashes the heads of two nuns together and they fall down, slapstick-style. 'What is the very nature of truth?'

'The dictionary defines truth as the conformity to fact or reality.' I take out the kneecaps of a nun who's brandishing a pump action shotgun.

'That's exactly the point,' says Sue, kicking another nun square in the crotch. She goes down with a smile on her face. 'Kieran knows no boundaries to truth or reality. He can literally stretch the reality around us.'

'Trust me, sister,' I say, as I take out a ninja who's crawling across the ceiling. He falls onto four other ninjas, knocking them out. 'This is a normal working day for me.'

'The truth is, I have every connection with Kieran you could possibly think of,' says Sue, blasting a ninja who's dressed as a pantomime cow. 'He stretches the infinite realities around him and weaves whatever spell he wants from them, and I've seen all my past existences.'

'You're not making sense, doll,' I say, cold cocking a nun disguised as a wall.

'You need to bone up on your theoretical quantum mechanics concerning a multiverse reality,' shouts Sue, shooting a squad of ninjas a mean looking stare that sends them running away like girls.

'I need to bone up on some one-on-one interaction with these jokers and my fists.' I demonstrate this theory by knocking down several rabid nuns with a few good right hooks. 'If you've seen every one of your past realities with Kieran, then isn't this just another one?' I spot an exit. 'Through there!'

We crash through into the next room—a vast overgrown docking bay with two huge water tanks, both housing state of the art submarines.

And this one's full of nuns and ninjas too.

'That's why Kieran wants me taken out of the picture,' says Sue, flipping a ninja over the guard-rail and sending him screaming into the water below. 'I found out he jumps between all those eternal realities and uses them to get my good looking ass out of his grasp.'

'Then how come he landed you with the penguins?' I emphasise my question by taking out a few nuns.

'He's stronger than me,' says Sue, looking lost, but only

after she's bitch-slapped some ninjas. 'He found out what I was doing and put a lock on my ability to leapfrog around the different existences. I've still got some talent left, but it's finite. I've spent most of it getting you out of trouble.'

'I make my own trouble, sister,' I mutter, and just then the wall behind us explodes and the Mother Superior comes raging out into the docking bay, five times her normal size and screaming blue murder.

EIGHTY NINE

She's on the rampage. Tossing her minions to left and right, the fire of the Lord in her eyes and a big chunk of steel in her hand.

'Nun smash!' she roars and starts lumbering over towards us, scattering everyone in her path.

'The subs!' I yell. Sue spins out a blaze of fire behind her, trying to take out the kneecaps, but it doesn't do any good. I kick a nun off the ladder leading down to the nearer sub and we scramble down.

'Return to your Mother Superior!' screams the penguin, enraged, and grabs the ladder, wrenching it backwards and forwards. I sling an arm around a rung and catch hold of Sue as she loses her grip and starts to fall.

'Time to take the big dive,' I shout, and we jump the last twenty feet and scramble towards the sub's hatch.

As I spin the hatch wheel, Sue goes straight for the sub's main cannon, an ugly piece of steel holding six inch shells. She spins it around and aims straight for the Mother Superior's head.

'Genuflect in front of this!' she snarls, and blasts off a shot. The head nun ducks and the shell knocks a hole in the roof.

'Get in!' I've got the hatch open and we scramble inside.

Driving a sub's just like driving a car—just a lot harder to pick up chicks with.

I jam the sub into gear and it groans and screeches and backs off out of the bay. Sue's at the periscope and she doesn't look happy. 'She's gaining on us!'

'Better load up a torpedo,' I mutter as we sail back towards the closed doors.

'The sub won't make it!' Sue looks panicked, but this isn't the first time I've been in this kind of situation.

'Get me some grens,' I tell her, and she searches around the hold until she uncovers a sack of pineapples just waiting for the pins to be pulled. 'Better get out of here, sister. This could get messy.'

She scoots up the ladder as I race down to the torpedo deck and pull the pins on the grenades. I make it back onto the sub's deck as it drifts gently towards the end of the docking bay.

The Mother Superior's still raging against the machine, picking up a generator and tossing it against the wall.

We dive into the water and head for the nearest piece of dry metal. Sue's up and out, popping off nuns like it's her birthday.

The sub crashes against the doors of the docking bay and the whole thing goes up in a blinding explosion that knocks everyone off their feet, except the Mother Superior.

'Nun Kill!' she shouts, and heads towards us stomping everyone in her path, nuns and ninjas alike begging for mercy as her huge feet come crashing down on them.

The sub explosion has blown a hole in the wall. I grab Sue and we hightail it out of there and into the desert, water from the docking bay sloshing around us, the head nun still raging after us.

'She's impossible to stop!' screams Sue. 'She's like a force of nature! She's one of Kieran's most successful experiments.'

'And she's wearing the building.' I aim for the pivotal nail in the structure and pop off a shot. It spins out, and the whole building starts to shake.

The Mother Superior starts to flail at the debris as it falls down around her. With a grinding heave the whole building gives up the ghost and collapses on top of her.

'That won't stop her,' says Sue.

'It's not meant to,' I say. 'But it should keep her down long enough that we can get on with the case.'

'What case, Mr Fury?' says a voice behind me, and I turn to see a suave businessman in a suit, smoking the finest Havana known to man. 'The only case you'll be looking at if you go for that popgun will be a casket.'

NINETY

'What the hell are you babbling about, Mac?' I yell, taking a bead on his crotch. 'Speak now or forever hold your nuts.'

The businessman laughs in a self-satisfied way and swaggers over towards us. 'You mistake my rather individual sense of humour, you moronic rectal breach.'

I'm lining up to take his jawbone down when he slaps an arm around my shoulders. 'Money is an interesting object, isn't it, Mr Fury?'

'Depends who's holding the clip,' I say. 'Now scotch me a cigar and let's talk business.'

'Come into my parlour, said the spider to the fly.' The businessman snorts laughter through his nose.

'You have my permission to kick his nads into outer space when this is over,' I mutter to Sue as we're led away.

NINETY ONE

A short trip later and we're whisked into the offices of OmniShyte Corp, a huge, black towering skyscraper on the edge of the road.

'Don't worry about your car, Mr Fury,' smarms the businessman. 'OmniShyte will take care of everything.'

We enter the foyer—plush and clean with polished floors—and head straight into a lift. It shoots up to the top floor and opens to reveal a businessman's paradise.

The office is more like the garden of earthly delights, even down to the half-naked chicks lolling about eating grapes. It's got waterfalls, plush couches, divans, a small orchestra playing a selection of classics in the corner of the room, and soap in the toilets.

'Now, Mr Fury, you've been through a trial recently,' says the businessman.

'If you're looking to deal, we need a shot of the good stuff first, Mr . . .'

The businessman laughs. 'Aha. Of course. My name. Some call me Alucard. Some call me Nomed. Some call me Natas. But you can call me whatever you like, as long as it's not for dinner.'

I'm lining up to blow his jawbone away when Sue waves me down.

'Sorry, sorry,' mutters the businessman. 'My little joke. My name's actually Charles. Charles MadeUpName. Part of the famous MadeUpName dynasty.'

'Is this some kind of joke?' I take the bourbons off him, hand one to Sue and knock mine back. Good stuff. The best.

'You've seen through my clever disguise.' I glance at the paperwork on the nearest desk. It actually says 'From the desk of Charles MadeUpName—OmniShyte.'

'Never heard of OmniShyte,' I tell him, knocking back another snifter to bring some life to my brain. 'They deal in stocks and shares or just hot air?'

'Your wit is amazing,' says Charles. 'No, no, we deal in the best commodity of all—futures. Well, specifically, your future.'

'This better be worth the trip,' I say. He offers me a seat and I take it.

'I'm a successful man, Mr Fury. I can buy and sell anything, everyone, and everything that was ever owned by anyone, and I have an offer for you.'

'What's the catch?'

'No catch. Just a watch.'

'Which watch?'

Charles nods to my pocket. I take out the stop watch the monk gave me in the land of the endless wars and hold it up.

'Such a watch,' mutters Charles, and I can see the misty look in his eyes.

'Why do you want this antique?' I ask. 'It's not worth anything.'

'Let's not kid ourselves, Mr Fury,' says Charles. 'I know the value of the watch and I know what it can do. I know it's a vortex into the netherworld.'

'Netherworld,' I mutter. 'That some kind of lingerie shop?'

Charles springs to his feet, all anger and bluster. 'Hell, Mr Fury. It's the gateway into Hell!'

'Nice work, stooge,' I nod. 'But what would you want with it?'

'I merely require it for my collection.' Charles gets himself back together and turns towards a vast cupboard beside the far window. 'Follow me.'

I do.

He throws open the doors. Inside are all kinds of trinkets and antiques. Some look like junk, but others sparkle with the taste of money.

'For instance, look at this.' Charles picks up a D-cup from a bra. 'This was the original Holy Grail.' He grasps a small model airplane shaped like a lump of concrete. 'The original design for the Spruce Goose. And trust me, Mr Fury, it *could* fly.'

'Got anything that doesn't suck?' Sue walks up behind us. She's not convinced. 'Anything we can trade?'

Charles smiles obsequiously at her and picks up a plastic bag. 'Try this on.'

'What the hell is that supposed to do?'

Charles just smiles at her. Then money starts to pour out of the bag, spilling onto the floor. 'Not bad, eh?'

'Nice collection, but the watch isn't up for sale.' I knock back the rest of the whisky and head for the exit. 'Call me when you've managed to extract your head from your rectum and we'll snatch a Mickey Finn sometime.'

'Wait, Mr Fury!' I turn to look at him. 'Perhaps I can persuade you with this?' And he pulls out a rocket launcher and aims it straight for my head.

NINETY TWO

'Drop the water pistol, Mac,' I tell him. 'Or we're talking some serious recompense.'

'I'm serious, Mr Fury.' Charles edges a finger over the trigger. 'Hand over that watch.'

I walk towards him. 'What do you really want it for?'

'I want it for me.' He's trying to sound crazed, but his eyes are totally sane. 'I want to be able to travel to Hell and back. I have a late aunt who owes me money.'

'Your gags aren't getting any better, Charles.' I stare him square in the eye. 'Now take a hike.'

I turn and start walking. I hear the rocket launcher drop and Charles is suddenly in front of me, on his knees, pleading.

'Please, please, please, I really need it.' He glances over his shoulder. There's a big, black cloud gathering in the sky, full of lightning bolts. 'I've spent my whole life building OmniShyte up. I can't lose it just for this. I need that watch.'

'Kieran put you up to this?' I ask.

'He's tried everything else—all the combat and fury—and now there's nothing but negotiation.'

'He should have tried that at the start.' I wave Charles out of the way and head for the elevator. 'Come on, Sue, let's hit the road.'

The cloud suddenly sweeps forwards, blanketing the building and plunging the outside world into darkness. A lightning bolt streaks out and crashes into the windows, blowing them out.

'This isn't good,' says Charles with a squeak, and he gets up and scrambles over to the rocket launcher. He picks it up and swings it towards the cloud. 'Eat rocket shaped death you totalitarian ass muncher!'

The rocket streaks off into the cloud and explodes. Suddenly the cloud reaches out with a huge, misty, grey hand and plucks Charles straight off the floor.

'Tell my money I loved it,' he shrieks at me as he's whisked past and disappears into the cloud. We hear screams, cries and a few guttural howls, then it's over.

'I think it's time we got out of here,' says Sue, as a flying pirate ship smashes through the glass and comes straight for us.

NINETY THREE

'Avast, me hearties, shiver me timbers and splice the mainbrace,' says the captain as he reaches down and plucks Sue off the ground. 'Time for me supper, arrrr.'

I've had enough of pirates. I pull out the popgun and take out the rudder with a few well placed shots, then start running as the flying ship heads towards the opposite end of the room. It starts to list, the bow edges down and it crashes through the window, straight for the desert below. I leap on to the deck and grab Sue.

'If you're stepping out of reality then now's the time to do it,' I yell. Behind us the cloud spills down, the giant hand reaching out for us. I brace myself and leap off the ship, pumping round after round into the cloud as we fall. Sue manages to snap off a few clips from her Uzi as the ground comes rushing up to greet us.

NINETY FOUR

We land in the desert, but it isn't by the road. In the distance are the pyramids, rising into the sky, all lined up symmetrically. Egyptian architects stand around, directing hordes of people, but they don't look like slaves. No one's pulling slabs of stone and no one looks oppressed.

'I think the history books lied to us,' says Sue.

'Either that or we were misinformed.' I hear a thunderous roar behind me and glance around to see the Sphinx heading in our direction, its concrete limbs shedding dust as it hammers towards us.

I pull out the cannon and the Sphinx grinds to a halt, kicking up sand over both of us.

'No need for the popgun, honey,' says the Sphinx, and it has a surprisingly mellow, feminine voice. 'I'm not your enemy.' She flicks her tail at the pyramids. 'Want to see how they *really* moved them.'

The ground shakes and shudders and one of the pyramids tilts, sways, and suddenly lurches upwards on two huge stone feet. It takes a few steps sideways, sending everyone reeling around like they're on the deck of a ship, then it sinks back down onto the ground.

'No one ever believes that kind of thing could happen,' the Sphinx tells me. 'No one's got the imagination to see the truth right in front of their eyes.'

'So what's the deal, sugar?' I ask her, shoving the popgun back into my jacket. 'What are we doing here?'

'You're after Kieran, aren't you?' she says, and I nod. 'Thought so. I could feel the rumblings through the time lines.'

'If you're about to start banging on about quantum mechanics you can forget it,' I tell her. 'Right now I need out of this joint and over to Kieran's.'

'We've all got our passage to follow, honey,' says the Sphinx. 'Don't knock it. And besides, all this crap about quantum mechanics and reality shifts is nothing but smoke and mirrors.'

Sue doesn't look pleased. 'But Kieran told me—'

'Kieran told you a lie, honey.' The Sphinx spares her a sympathetic look. 'He can hoodwink with whatever "facts" he thinks are appropriate. It's all baloney at the end of the day. You, of all people, should know there are no facts—just perceptions.'

Sue looks like her world has been shattered. She slumps to the ground and puts her head in her hands.

'I should have known,' she whispers.

'Don't let it deflate your oyster, babes,' says the Sphinx. 'We've all suffered from his bullshit at one point or another.' She looks up at the sky. 'Come with me—I'll give you a whistle stop around the provinces.'

'I got no time for sightseeing, doll,' I tell her. 'I'm on a case.'

'I'm not talking about Egypt, you numpty,' she says. 'I'm talking about time.' And suddenly we're in London.

NINETY FIVE

In a back lane. It's dark and gloomy and there's crap all over the place. A small man with a curly moustache, a big hat and a firelighter walks up to a small tinderbox.

'He can't see us,' the Sphinx tells us. 'Or maybe he can. I'm not sure. Anyway, the books will have you believe the Great Fire of London was started by accident. And they were sort of right.'

A shadowy leg sticks out and trips the man up. The firelighter falls on the tinderbox and the whole thing goes up.

'Of course, nothing is ever real or not real.' The Sphinx regards me as I spark up a Havana from the flames.

'I think I've heard enough about whatever the hell reality is, toots,' I tell her. 'I get the feeling nothing's tangible any more, and I don't need any kind of history lesson. It's all written by the winners, and the facts get distorted—and all reality is the product of whoever the hell is experiencing it in the first place anyway, so let's cut the sideshows and get moving. I've got Kieran to bring in.'

'But I've got so much to show you,' says the Sphinx, and we're off again.

NINETY SIX

And we're in the White House. Nixon, Reagan and Kennedy are huddled around a table, with Nixon pointing at several land masses on a map. It's not hard to see what their eventual aim is from the tanks and helicopters lined up on the map.

'Yeah, we get the gist, sister.' I puff smoke in her direction. 'We've already met these jokers.'

'They're just part of the problem,' says the Sphinx. 'I can take you to the people who they think are controlling them.'

'Will it help the case?'

'You be the judge of that.' And she whisks us up through the roof and we're in a giant boardroom, seating twenty three, and every seat is filled by some bigwig in a business suit hammering the table.

'I got the funk and I need to feel it!' screams one of the figures.

'Take me to your leader, earthling butt pirates!' screams another.

'Man, this jig is wasted on you fools,' shouts a third.

'Let me guess,' I say. 'The Illuminati.'

'It's whatever you want it to be,' says the Sphinx. 'That's the beauty of it. Kieran picked the dumbest minds in the world to help govern the universe, because it is, after all, made up of mutable facts and twisted reality. And what you see before your eyes every day of your life is just what you select.'

'Well, I see some pretty strange things,' I tell her.

'You've got a bit more insight and vision than most people.' The Sphinx smiles down at me. 'You see the gaps which people don't see.'

'You're forgetting one thing.' I take a puff on the cigar. 'I'm a P.I. That's all I ever was and that's all I ever am. I don't hold no mystical powers, mystical sources or strange abilities to alter reality or facts or whatever the hell you want to hoodwink people with.'

'And that makes you one in a million,' explains the Sphinx. 'Everyone else in the world does to some extent. But they don't know it.'

'Okay, enough of the exposition. I've got a job to do.'

'As you wish.'

And we're back in the desert with the burning shell of Om-niShyte behind us sending plumes of black smoke curling into the air.

'Where am I? Back at square one?'

'Your journey has been full of surprises,' says the Sphinx. 'But there's still a hill to climb.' And with that she's gone.

'Well, that babe was a barrel of laughs,' I say to Sue, but she just looks at me with saucer eyes. 'What's scratching your hump?'

'She's opened you up to the truth—'

'Don't you start.' And I get in the shark and gun the engine. Sue crawls in beside me and we tear off down the strip.

'Don't you see what she was saying?' Sue says, almost pleading.

'I don't need to see what she's saying.' I shake my head. 'I've said it before and I'll say it again, all a man needs is a whisky, a good cigar and a car, and that's what I got. Questioning the laws of reality is for schmucks.'

'But you're—*Watch out!*'

NINETY SEVEN

She warns me just in time. I slam on the brakes and squeal to a halt inches away from a group of armed guards holding big, mean, ugly weapons. One of them jogs around to my side.

'State the purpose of your visit!'

I scan the area. Part of it is locked off. Stands in the far distance. Something big and shiny pointing up into the sky. A pre-fab building a few miles away from it.

'Professor Sparks,' I tell the guard, whipping out a fake ID and flashing it under his nose. He scans the ID and nods.

'We've been expecting you.' He stands back and gestures. 'If you'd like to step out of the car we'll escort you to the launch area.'

I nod and a jeep pulls up. Soon we're outside the pre-fab building.

The guard leads us into a room full of computers and data banks, with people in white shirts and black slacks rushing around like their lives depended on looking like computer pro-grammers.

119

The guard salutes and leaves us, and some guy with a crew cut and a stern but friendly look walks over and shakes our hands.

'Professor Sparks,' I tell him, and he looks askance and nods, then gestures to the giant viewing screen dominating the room.

'I'm glad you got here in time, Prof,' he says. 'We're just about to launch the shuttle.' Crew Cut turns to the nerds. 'Start the countdown.'

I walk towards the viewing screen. Framed dead centre is a space shuttle, but there's something different about this one. Something strange.

Sue sidles up beside me. 'This smells bad. Something is about to go wrong.'

It does. Big style.

The boosters kick in and the shuttle takes off, leaving a trail of fire. It barely gets a few hundred feet off the ground before the wings buckle in. Everyone panics. Lots of shouting, running, punching buttons; but nothing's doing any good.

The wings punch back out and shape themselves into giant steel claws, jutting from the sides of the main body. The shuttle curves around in an arc as missile launchers and machine guns pop out from under the wings. The front end buckles and twists and transforms into a giant grinning, razor-toothed, red-eyed face.

'This could be a good time to leave,' I say. Sue nods, but it's too late.

The shuttle creature screams straight at the stands and starts blasting away with everything, sending missiles curving towards the people streaming away from the area. Bullets tear up the ground around the fleeing crowds. This is one ugly scene.

A few guards start taking pot shots back, but they get torn up and thrown away by the machine gun fire.

The shuttle swoops down and picks up a tank, then sends it hurtling back down to the ground where it explodes in a giant fireball.

'I got a good idea who's responsible for this.' I turn to Sue. 'Get back to the shark, toots, and be there when I need you.' And I'm off.

NINETY EIGHT

I blast into the stairwell and tear up to the roof door. It's locked, but a few swift kicks and I'm out.

The shuttle creature is off in the distance, but it seems to know I'm there. It crawls around in a not-so-graceful arc and heads right for me.

There's no substitute for a well aimed shot, so I pull out my cannon and aim straight for the eagle eyes. The shuttle starts to shift and dodge, and it's quick, but not quick enough.

I blast off a shot, which whacks into the metal shell and ricochets away into nowhere. I didn't figure on this. I pump more rounds towards the creature, hoping for a lucky hit, but today isn't going to grow any orchids for me.

The shuttle creature homes in and the wings hunch down as it streams towards me, blasting everything it has. The roof of the building turns into a nightmare of fire and spinning debris behind me. I know it's got its range wrong and any moment now it'll adjust and that'll be that, and I'll be roasting on the bad side along with Chicago and his boys.

I start running at the creature because there's nothing else I can do. It locks in on me and the machine guns and rocket launchers adjust as it screams closer and closer. At the last second I leap high and far into the air as the creature ploughs into the building.

I manage to catch one of the metal plates on the back of the shuttle as it tears through the building and away, and I yank myself forwards, plate over plate, until I'm staring down at its control room.

A few close up shots hammer through the material. A hole opens up and I'm inside.

It's mechanical, but there's a pulsing brain stuck all over the vital components. I look up and the sky turns blue and then black and suddenly there's stars all around me.

It's either fight now or fly, so I punch a fist into the nearest brain matter and yank out a handful. The shuttle judders and jerks and I rip out another handful and throw it behind me.

The shuttle keeps going, though, and as it hits the outer atmosphere a membrane seals over the hole in the shell, but I still keep hammering away at the brain until it's nothing but

pulped, blasted matter at my feet, and the controls are mine.
Except we're high up.

Ladies and gentlemen, we are floating in space.

NINETY NINE

And if that isn't bad enough, there's a big, mean, ugly looking spaceship heading straight towards me. It's like a slab of
metallic meat with pincers on the end. And they're coming
right for me.

'Hand over your ship to the forces of Imperium,' a voice
booms out over the communications system, 'or we shall crush
you like the fly you are.'

Good enough reason to fight back.

I search around the controls and try to find something to
blast the ship out of the sky with. Eventually I hook on a red
warning button.

I slam a fist on it and missiles pour out, pummelling a line
of small explosions along the front of the spaceship. I grab the
controls, hit the boosters and send the shuttle into a barrel roll
as a stream of missiles come for me.

They're heat seekers and they're locked on to their mark.
Just one thing for it. I kick the shuttle up and take it into a
wide curving spin, leading the missiles into a chase, then head
straight back towards the spaceship. Straight for the launch
bay.

The ship spews out smaller battle craft. I pull the shuttle
up at the last moment and the missiles slam into the launch
bay and take out the rest of their fleet in rolling, blooming
explosions which tear a big, jagged gash in the side of the
craft.

But the small battle craft are after me. There's no forma-
tion, so I figure there's nothing but idiots behind the controls.

I send the shuttle into a sideways spin that brings two of the
battle craft slamming together into a pleasant fireball. Another
craft hooks on my tail and starts to trace my moves, blasting
out shots that rip into one of the wings and stitch a line up the
back of the shuttle.

The giant spaceship looms in front of me, fire still spilling
out from the launch bay. Battle craft start to close in on all

sides. As far as I can tell there's no way out, so I crunch down on the speed and boost the thrusters to max, then start hammering the big red button.

Missiles stream out and tear up what's left of the launch bay, punching further into the craft, destroying everything in their path and ripping a hole through the spaceship. I reach the first explosion and keep on going.

The missiles strip a small but straight line through the giant spaceship and blow a hole out the other side. As I emerge from the explosion, I take a glance in the rear monitor and watch as the smaller craft get caught in the giant fireball as the craft goes up. Everything gets torn into next year's memories.

I sit back in the chair and light up a cigar, taking my time to savour the taste as the shuttle rattles with the force of the explosions.

'Maybe that'll teach you not to mess with Joe Fury,' I say to the monitor. A blinding light hits the shuttle and suddenly I'm not there anymore.

ONE HUNDRED

Instead I'm in a white room and there's a vague indistinct figure at the edge of the light.

'What's the deal?' I ask.

'No deal.' The voice is soft and mellow. 'Your craft was breaking up. I am merely rescuing you from the destruction.'

'Thanks, Mac,' I say, puffing on the cigar. 'To what do I owe this honour?'

'I am the one who owes you the honour,' says the figure. 'I am Kevin, mind god of the planet you call "Earth" and lead singer of the popular band, "The Scrotal Sacks".'

'I'm sure you make a great noise,' I say. 'You got the power to get me down to the ground.'

'Certainly,' says Kevin. 'But first I must question you. It is not so often I get to meet a man such as yourself.'

I figure I owe him that much for saving my life. 'Okay, fire away, but make it snappy. I'm on a case.'

And suddenly we're sitting down in glowing white chairs while Kevin, albino white and also glowing, slips me a sharp whisky on the rocks. 'I believe it is to your taste, Mr Fury.'

I'm getting used to people knowing my name. 'The pleasure's all mine.'

'Now, Mr Fury, first I must congratulate you on a marvellous victory over the evil Overlords. The sanctimonious fascists have always been a problem for the rest of the universe.'

'If one ship and a handful of fighters are enough to be a problem for the universe, then the universe is in pretty rough shape.'

'Ha ha ha.' Kevin pronounces every syllable. He settles back in his chair. 'So what drove you into being a private detective?'

'The usual,' I tell him. 'The whisky's cheap and the hours are short.'

'What were you before becoming a private eye?'

'A citizen of the world,' I tell him. 'And if you don't like that, a citizen of the local bar. I find I do my best work under a neon beer light.'

'Very witty,' says Kevin. 'And what is the toughest case you have ever encountered?'

'They're all tough.' I lean back in my chair and take a puff on the cigar. 'Except the ones that aren't. But they're few and far between.'

'And would you say you have an engaging personality?'

'I've never been engaged, if that's what you're asking,' I say. 'If you don't count my job, that is.'

'Very dry,' laughs Kevin. 'But we wish to know more.'

Something wrong here. 'Who's "we"?'

'Oh dear,' says Kevin, looking sheepish. 'I appear to have let the warthog out of the splooge.'

And the light snaps off and Kevin isn't glowing any more. And neither is anything else.

'Bollocks!' snaps Kevin. 'Sorry, mate. Look, can we do that again but without that bloody question? I stuffed it right up the Khyber.'

'Okay, buster, where the hell am I and what's going on?'

'Right, well, I can see you need an explanation, so hold onto your knackers me old cheese pie. It's time to take you back into "The Land That Knobends Forgot".' And the ground opens up, a light shoots down to the lush green Earth spinning in infinite space, and we're propelled down the beam into a dark, dingy lab stuffed full of leaking pipes and body parts.

'Sorry about that, mate,' says Kevin. 'Mind if we cut all your limbs off, pickle your brains, put yer todger on display and then slap your bum on the evening news? This is showbiz.'

And that's when I pull the gun out.

ONE HUNDRED AND ONE

'Hold up, hold up,' pleads Kevin, holding his hands out defensively. 'No need to get your bollocks in a twist. It was only a joke.'

'The mutilation or the showbiz?'

'The mutilation.'

'I outta plug ya right here,' I snarl, and he backs off some more.

'Hold yer horses, mate,' he says in a bad cockney accent. 'We're just feeding the media machine, alright?'

'You can cut the accent too, Van Dyke,' I tell him, stepping forward. He backs off and comes up against a wall of machinery. 'That mockney just makes me see red.'

'Okay,' he says, dropping the comedy cockney. 'Sorry about that old chap, but your rep precedes you. When I saw the old bish bosh gun battle up there in the stratos, it was too good an opportunity to miss to nab you for a bit of an old chinwag.'

'I think I preferred the mockney.' I holster the weapon. 'What's this whole get up, anyway.'

'This is where we churn out the old showbiz machine, my good man.' Kevin starts to walk around the place, which is stuffed with jars of body parts, and what looks like a big sandwich toaster at the far end of the room. 'We chuck the bits and pieces in one end, program the old personality, and Fanny's your bellend.'

He walks over to a board of lights and switches. 'Look, see here. We can type in a bit of hype.' He starts bashing away at the keyboard and flipping switches. 'Chuck in some rags to riches sob stories, some victimisation at school—that kind of thing. The usual "crying myself to sleep" at night, as though the vacuous toads haven't heard of the real world out there. Maybe a little dab of imperfection on the features—nose too big, neck too thick.' He pushes a big red button. 'That's the old vanity drive. Chuck a steaming great wadge of these babies in, and suddenly the old duffers have more ego than your average soap star convention.'

Lights start to flash and the toaster whirrs and blows out a hiss of steam. It opens, revealing a bemused looking woman in a silky robe and too much make-up, blinking against the lights.

'It's all a bit disconcerting at first, but they get used to it.' Kevin leans towards the new arrival. 'How are you feeling, Jizzelda?'

The woman blinks, spots him, and staggers over. She's already decked out in twelve inch heels.

'Gorsh, it's simply delightful,' splutters the woman in an English accent that could cut glass. Then something strange happens. She jerks her head and twitches. 'Ma daddy used ta beat us with a stick until we criiiiied all night.' Straight from the boondocks.

Kevin sighs and pulls out a Desert Eagle. He doesn't even look when he pops the woman in the forehead. She goes down in a heap and a brace of ducks with feather dusters waddle out from under the machine and clear away the mess.

'Of course sometimes we get it wrong.'

'Okay, Fauntleroy, I've heard enough.' I start looking round for the exit, but there's nothing but banks of machinery everywhere. 'How do I get out of this joint?'

'With my help, old bean,' says Kevin, swivelling around to look at me. 'I have an option for you.'

'You can option my fist if you like,' I say, stepping forward.

Kevin laughs. 'That's one of the reasons we love you, old man.' He pats me on the shoulder, then placates me with a shot of whisky and a fine pack of Havanas. 'I don't *need* anything from you and I don't want to *take* anything from you. I just need you to hold something for me. And it's not even heavy.'

'Fire away.' The whisky and the cigar taste good.

Kevin waves away the smoke. 'The media has always been pushed by events in the news, and contrary to popular belief, always been driven by celebrity shite. Any moron who tells you that in the good old days serious news was King is talking out of their hairy old rectums. People want celebrity shite, and we give the bastards what they want. Now we've got all kinds of modern devices to feed this bilge directly into the sub-cortex and get people dribbling their brains straight out of their arseholes. It's a wizard scam, a cracking wheeze, and an almighty way of feeding acres of plop to the willing public.'

'Nice speech. What's that got to do with me?'

'Well, funny you should ask, old boy.' Kevin sits down and tent-poles his fingers. 'We've been hearing about this bally old adventure you've been having with Kieran.'

'You know about Kieran?'

'Everyone who should know does know.'

'And what about it?'

'We were wondering if you'd like to wear a camera and broadcast your adventures to the willing public.'

'A twenty four hour Kieran cam.' I take a deep puff on the cigar.

'It's small and unobtrusive,' Kevin tells me. 'Basically we can plug it into your jacket pocket or something and broadcast whatever you do.'

'What's in it for me?'

'Fame, fortune, money, success.' Kevin smiles. 'The chance to get out there in the public eye and become a celebrity.'

I blow smoke in his face. 'No deal.'

Kevin stares at me, uncomprehending, and then— 'No, listen, you don't understand. It's a chance to become a celebrity.'

'Why would I want to do that?'

'Because everyone does, dammit!' Kevin's out of his chair and storming towards me. A flick of the popgun stops him in his tracks. 'It's the height of achievement for anyone. People *like* you—they want to be like you, they want to be around you, they want to nosh on your naughty bits and let you do squirmy things to their genitalia. It's what everyone in this whole damn world should be aiming for, and only a freak or a maladjusted solitaricist would even think of turning down an opportunity to enrich their life like this. It's the pinnacle of all human ambition, the greatest aim in existence—the wonderful, sugar-coated, sequinned world of *celebrity!*'

I stare him clear in the eye. He looks hopeful. There's a smile on his face. And we stay like that for a while. Then Kevin's face starts to fall when he realises I'm not hooked to his game.

'Don't you want that?'

'You're a viper, Kevin.' The barrel of the gun wavers towards his forehead. 'Show me the way out of here, or I'll ventilate your cranium.'

Kevin backs up to one of the machines and starts to fumble about. Warning buzzers sound and I figure it's a good time to get out of here.

No point plugging the wimp, so I run towards one of the walls and start looking for an exit. But there's nothing except computers on all sides.

One of them starts to slide aside and the horrors of Kevin's celebrity experiments pour out into the room. All the wrong experiments by the look of things. Everything Kevin couldn't bring himself to put down with a bullet. A mass of limbs and bug eyes and collagened lips and oversized busts and pumped up abs.

'Get him!' screams Kevin. I spot a security camera and a bullet takes out the clamp holding it to the wall.

'Sweet dreams, Poindexter!' I catch the camera as it falls and throw it over the mutants' heads, straight at Kevin. It knocks him on the head and he's on his knees, bloodied and confused.

The celebrity freaks break off from chasing me and stream towards the camera; a primping, preening mass. Kevin picks it up and shakes away the cloud from his head, but by then it's too late. As far as the freaks are concerned, Kevin *is* the camera. They tear him to pieces trying to get into the limelight.

I hike through the gap where the mutants emerged, then through corridors lined with a thousand screens, all buzzing a different channel, and blow open the far door. I'm out into the desert again next to the road and breathing in the fresh air.

Sue comes screeching up in the shark and slides to a halt in front of me.

'What kept you so long?' I ask.

'We got a problem.' She nods behind her and I see what she means. It's a biggie.

ONE HUNDRED AND TWO

It's not just the nuns. It's not just the ninjas. It's not even just Molesto the King of the Sheep. Everything we've met during the whole damn trip is coming right at us.

Sue throws me a pair of binoculars. 'Hop in and take a look. I'll drive.'

I don't argue with her, I just climb into the back seat. She fires up the engine and we fishtail away from the horde and head off down the road.

I peer through the binocs and scan the crowd. Familiar faces—all the bad guys you could ever want. But no Preston and no Mother Superior. The giant talking ninja chickens and Chicago and his Hell-spawn friends are missing from the mix as well, but then they were always on our side.

'We're missing a few bad guys and all of the good ones,' I say to Sue.

'I noticed. Looks like the hounds have finally come to take a bite out of us.'

I load ammo into the popgun and aim at the approaching mob. 'Not if I've got anything to do with it.'

But they're too far away to do any damage. Most of them are coming after us in battered, dilapidated trucks, cars and patchwork vehicles. Everything I didn't destroy or mutilate has been shaken up and turned into something with wheels.

'Better keep your foot down or we're somebody's breakfast.' I turn back to face the way ahead.

'I think we've used up our lucky chips,' says Sue nodding at the gas gauge. We're almost out.

'Crap.' I look up at the way ahead and Kieran's compound is visible, but a good way off.

Getting closer on our left is a dilapidated old diner. It looks like it's open.

'Time to make a last stand.' I nod towards the diner and Sue flips the wheel into a spin and we slide to a halt by the front door.

'Better lock and load,' I tell her, but she's already there.

ONE HUNDRED AND THREE

Inside we slam the door and bar it with whatever we can find. The waitress, middle aged and with bad make-up, looks confused as I race through the kitchen, past the startled cook and over to the back door. Solid. I slam it shut and then head for the pots and pans.

'Cook 'em up. Quick.' I start emptying cooking oil into the pans. 'We've got a major league problem heading this way.'

The cook nods and then starts filling the pans with anything that burns, including the cigarette in his mouth.

I dash out into the main area and Sue's stacking everything she can lay her hands on up against the windows.

'Doesn't look good,' she says, propping herself against the glass and snapping the chamber back in the Uzi. 'Could be the final stand.'

'Don't give up 'til it's worth it,' I tell her. 'There's always a way out of these things.'

The crowd surges around the diner, nuns first, and soon they've got the place surrounded. But they don't try to break in. Something's wrong. Or maybe right.

'Bloody hell!' The cook comes out, sparking another cigarette. 'I knew this would happen one day.' He gestures at me. 'Are you that Joe Fury the people keep talking about?'

'Yeah. What people?'

'Everyone. You're more famous than Death. And he's always bloody here.'

I nod to the crowd. 'Any idea what's going on around here?'

'Well, it looks to me as though the masses are revolting,' says the cook, and then refrains from the obvious joke.

'I think I know where we are,' says Sue, nodding at the bullet holes stitched into the walls and the table tops. 'I think this is where we started out.'

'That's right,' says the cook. 'It appears you've come full circle.'

'I would like to say that's impossible, but right now everything seems to be.' I stare back at the crowd.

'Well, not exactly full circle,' says the waitress. 'More like we've come to you. Or something like that. I know it's got something to do with reality shifts which don't actually exist.'

Suddenly the front door heaves, twitches and explodes inwards. The crowd outside take a step forward and then pause, straining against some invisible shield.

And that's when Preston and the Mother Superior step into the diner.

'Wanna negotiate?' says Preston with a smile.

ONE HUNDRED AND FOUR

'Let's take a seat,' I suggest, and we do. 'And if you give me any crap about alternate realities or quantum mechanics, I'll put a bullet in your head and take the consequences.'

'Say it ain't so, Joe,' Preston mocks. 'I'm not here to talk about theories or non-theories, Joe. I'm just here to talk.'

'Fire away.'

'You have a commodity which I would very much like to have.'

'I thought you wanted me to take down Kieran,' I say. 'Bring him in so you can sort him out.'

'The rules have changed slightly,' says Preston. 'Things are different. I didn't realise the monk gave you such a prize.'

'Why do you want the watch?'

'To negotiate with Kieran.' Preston sits back. 'Face it, Joe. You don't need it. You don't want it. It'll bring you nothing but pain and misery and problems.'

'What are you going to negotiate with Kieran about?' I light up a cigar.

'Delegation of duty,' says Preston, and there's a spark of anger in his eyes. 'Delegation of power. Life is all about sharing.'

'And you want some of what he's got?' I nod to Sue. 'What about the girl?'

'That's out of my jurisdiction.' Preston shakes his head. 'You'll have to talk with the Mother Superior.'

'Okay, penguin, what's the deal?'

Mother Superior coughs against the smoke and tries to smile. It's nice to see she's back to her normal size.

'Just return her to us—'

'No deal.' I pull out the gun and the pulsating crowd outside take a small step forward. 'What's to stop me plugging you right here and negotiating my way out with Preston.'

Her eyes glow red and angry. 'Only a thousand nuns, Mr Fury. Imagine that. Hunted down for the rest of your life by the power of the wimple. We are legion, Mr Fury.'

'You look like a zoo animal,' I tell her, and turn back to Preston. 'No negotiation until Sue gets a cut of the free life.'

'Forget the girl for the moment, Joe.' Preston's still trying to placate, but the anger's there and it's rising. He could probably do without the penguin throwing her wimple into the fire. 'Concentrate on the watch.'

'I don't believe a word of what you're saying. You've got a thousand forces out there gunning for my blood, and they could sweep in here and choke the watch out of us in a moment, but they're not. Something's keeping them back. And I think it's the watch.'

'And I intend to keep it out of the wrong hands and in the right ones,' says Preston.

'Okay, I gotta think about this.' I lean back in the seat. 'You got any whisky?' I shout to the waitress.

'Yeah, thanks!' she shouts back.

'Can you bring us out a few shots?'

She does, and we drink. As the liquid goes down, I pull out the stop watch and hold it up. Lust fills the eyes of Preston and the penguin. I hover my finger over the stop mechanism.

'What's to stop me pushing this right here and going back to my old friend Chicago?'

Preston looks down at me, and I suddenly realise he has the advantage. 'Because it doesn't work for you anymore. You've used your one and only go—'

'Cut the crap, Preston.' I take another slug of the good stuff. 'If that was the case you'd take me down now and run off with this baby.'

Preston's eyes go sour. He's been caught out.

I lean forward. 'Okay, the both of you. Shall we start again from the beginning? And this time I want the truth.'

That's when the cook turns up with a shotgun.

ONE HUNDRED AND FIVE

'I'm afraid I haven't been entirely honest with you, Mr Fury,' says the cook, cocking the shotgun. 'And I don't think you're entirely aware of what this place actually is.'

'You failed the health inspection?' I ask.

'Not exactly.' The cook nods to Preston. 'This boy here has been played for a sucker all along, and I don't think he even knows it. Mr Preston, you've never been out of Kieran's reach. I'm afraid he's been jerking your strings.'

'That's bullshit!' shrieks Preston, slamming a fist on the table. 'I'm in control of my life.'

'Really?' The cook couldn't have said it more sardonically. 'You—the nuns—the girl—all here at the same time. Too much of a coincidence, don't you think? Except Kieran made one fatal mistake. Choosing this place for the meet.'

'What's wrong with it?' says Preston.

'Well, for the last few thousand realities Kieran's been under the impression he's responsible for its existence,' says the cook. 'Unfortunately my old friend Chicago owns it. Which is one of the reasons those little spud balls out there can't get in. It's only testament to the strength of you and the Mother Superior that you managed to slip through the shield keeping the grockels out.'

Preston slams a fist on the table again. 'I knew it!' He turns to the cook. 'But that doesn't matter. They'll never get out. They're surrounded. They'll soon starve and that will be that, and then the watch will be mine.'

The cook smiles. 'Unfortunately for you it's been my duty to keep you talking until the cavalry arrives. Cheerio.'

The toilet doors blow off their hinges and the wall explodes as a giant, beefed up monster truck comes tearing through, ripping through the diner, taking out everything.

Chicago leans out of the driver's window. 'Need a lift?'

ONE HUNDRED AND SIX

We haul ourselves into the back, Chicago guns the engine and the truck screams off out of the diner, crashing through the other wall.

Behind us I see Preston and the Mother Superior get up and start running, but Chicago's put extra gas in this thing and he's maxed it out with everything he can.

'So long, losers!' he shouts out the window, tearing through the crowd surrounding the diner. Some of them scatter and some of them try to fight, and the popgun and the Uzi come out and we start nailing the bad guys. Most of them get the hint, forget about safety in numbers and scramble off out of the way and into the wilds.

The truck bounces over Molesto the King of the Sheep,

133

taking his head off, and it's plain sailing all the way down the road. We make it quick and fast, and anyone who wants a piece of us is left crying in the ditch as we race out of their range.

Kieran's compound looms up before us. Chicago cuts the engine and we idle slowly towards the main gate.

'This is as far as I can take you, Joe,' says Chicago. 'Even I can't get you past this barrier. It's hard enough keeping corporeal outside of Hell. I'm about to fade as it is.' He nods to the compound. 'We'd be in there like a shot if we could, but the building has a wall beneath, to the side and above to the people of Hell. Kieran's a tough customer, so watch out.'

We get out of the truck and scan the place. Gates are shut tight. 'No problem with that, Chicago.' I turn to him. 'See you on the flip side.'

Chicago nods and the ground opens up and swallows the truck.

The compound has a wall a hundred feet high, curving outwards and completely impossible to climb.

I spot the storm drain with the green tag on it that will lead us inside pretty easy. I take out the fork that Ginger gave me when he was repairing the spaceship, and jam it into the main lock on the compound's gates. Somewhere deep inside the fortress sirens wail. I have no idea how this will help, but Ginger's never let me down before.

The grid over the storm drain is locked solid and three inches thick, but I take the key that the joker from the vortex under the vampire's castle gave me and it fits like a glove. The grid opens with a clang and we start walking.

It's dark and wet, but it's a change from the dusty desert. I expect a longer walk, but fifteen minutes later we see the light seeping through a sewer grating.

'Act natural,' I say, and push the grating up.

The inside of the compound looks like a dusty city street. Buildings of all shapes, sizes and colours stretch off into the distance. If there's one thing I can say, it's that this place looks big. Too big.

And it's deserted.

'Bring back any memories?' I ask Sue as she crawls out of the drain. She looks around and shakes her head.

'It's different.' She shields her eyes for a better perspective. 'And there's no one around.'

A second later a steel cage clangs down around us and the hordes come out of the shadows.

ONE HUNDRED AND SEVEN

They drag us into a building in the middle of the compound. It's a post-modern mess—all bare boards and white walls.

The door opens and a man walks in. Tall, curly hair, glasses. He walks up to the cage and snorts. 'Good morning, Joe,' he says. 'Nice of you to break into my compound.'

'The pleasure's all mine,' I snarl, and the Poindexter laughs.

'You're a hard man,' says the geek, but his tone's serious and I know he means it. 'You are probably wondering who I am.'

'I know who you are, Kieran. Are you suffering from short term memory loss or something?' I leave the popgun and spark up a Havana. 'When are you gonna move us out of this cage?'

'All in good time,' mutters Kieran. 'Morning, Sue.'

Sue says nothing. She just looks at him. If the cage opens, Kieran's in danger of getting his balls chewed off.

'I've got a question, Kieran. Why all the fuss?'

'Fuss?'

'Why all the obstacles to stop us reaching you?' I puff smoke and cross my arms, fingers touching the butt of the gun. No point firing until we're out of this mess.

'They're tests,' says Kieran. 'I have to see if you're made of the right metal. If you want to join my army you need the right stuff.'

'I don't join anything unless they pay me.' I shift towards the door of the cage. Looks solid. 'Why don't you let us out and we'll take you to Preston and call it quits? After all, I've still got a case to close.'

Kieran clicks his fingers and the door of the cage opens and swings wide. 'Whatever you wish.'

I slip out the gun and pop off a shot, but Kieran holds out his hand and the cannon flies straight to him. The bullet slams into the wall behind him.

'Nice weapon.' Kieran throws the gun down.

'Let's make it one on one,' I say. 'You and me. If you win you can do what you want. If I win you're coming with me.'

Kieran looks at me and adjusts his glasses. 'The deal's on.'

Then he grabs his face and yanks it down, tearing the flesh off himself, pulling the skin down to reveal a man much bigger, much stronger. He's dressed in khaki pants and a green shirt, dog tags hanging from his neck, crew cut, eyes like diamonds, glaring daggers, hatred and pure anger straight at me.

'Whatever you want, Joe.' There's a sneer in his voice that I don't like the sound of.

I step out of the cage. He's big and ugly, but it's nothing I haven't seen before.

'You're on a downward spiral, Joe,' snarls Kieran. 'I am invincible.'

'So was the Roman empire.' And I swing for him, but he's not there any more. He's across the room, laughing.

'First you have to hit me.' Kieran strides forwards, getting close, and I square up. 'Why fight when we can talk?' he says.

'There's only so much room for jawing.' I swing for him again and he steps back and I'm hitting nothing but air.

'Why the anger, Joe?' Kieran starts to walk round me. 'All I want to do is talk.'

'Don't listen to him, Joe,' shouts Sue.

'We can just sit.' Kieran stops moving and there's no more hate in his eyes. 'Just sit and talk.'

'As long as there's whisky.'

ONE HUNDRED AND EIGHT

We're sitting in a living room, surrounded by art. The walls are caked with living legends. Sculptures fill every space that isn't taken up by the Arabian rug. It's like some sort of decadent fantasy.

'The case is off, Fury,' says Kieran, walking over to the drinks. 'Preston doesn't want me. He was under my influence all the while, but he didn't know it. I control him. Therefore, you've managed to reach me, therefore case closed.'

'What about the penguin?'

'She's independent. I gave you Sue to keep you on track for the compound if things got too surreal. The Mother Superior had to be kept in the dark so she wouldn't spill the beans. Like Preston. They're all my pawns. I *gave* you Sue.'

Kieran hands me the whisky. It's good.

'The best whisky you could possibly have,' he says, sitting down opposite me. 'Only the best.' He looks at me over the rim of his glass for a few seconds, then sets the drink down. 'You could have everything, Joe.'

'Are you trying to negotiate?'

'Yes.'

'No deal.'

'You could have everything, Joe,' says Kieran again, and he sips the whisky for emphasis. 'You made it all the way here, and I threw everything at you.'

'You didn't try hard enough.'

Kieran knocks back the rest of his whisky and stands up. 'I control the very nature of reality, Joe. I control everything you see and hear, and everything that happens to you. I can control your very fortune.'

'Nice words, but fill me up.' I hand him the glass and he does. Taking this chump isn't going to be easy without a few shots to kick start my engine.

'You could have everything,' says Kieran, and I get the feeling he's gearing up for a big speech. 'You could control the very—'

'Put a slice on it, wise guy,' I snap. 'Cut to the chase.'

Kieran slams me a look which tells me he likes my style. 'I want you to rule with me, Joe Fury. I want you by my side. I've thrown the world at you and you just keep coming back for more.'

'Chicago got me out of the last scrape.' I puff the stoogie and blow smoke on his dreams.

'That son of a bitch.' Kieran clenches his fists and walks round behind his chair. 'That no-good dirty son of a bitch.'

'You got a beef with him?' Nothing like stating the obvious.

'I won't lie to you, Joe,' lies Kieran. 'I need his fortune. He's the only man stopping me from bringing harmony to this land.'

'Harmony or problems?' I slip him a smile which doesn't reach my eyes.

'Harmony!' screams Kieran, and one of the priceless stat-

ues behind him explodes. He takes a deep breath and calms himself down.

'Hope that wasn't expensive,' I mutter.

'The only place I can't get to is Hell.' Kieran grabs the back of his seat and starts digging his nails in. 'Chicago runs that. And he can't get to me and I can't get to him. But if I got there myself, I could finally unleash my powers and take it over—make it a better place.'

'It's doing okay without you.'

'I need your watch, Joe.' Kieran walks over to me. 'I need your watch to take me to Hell. I know you've used your two goes, and it's ripe and ready for another use. I can use it. I can go into Hell and restore order.'

'Chicago helped me.' I stand up, toe to toe with Kieran. 'He pulled me out of the swamp, which means I owe him a favour. And the favour is not giving you the watch.'

I blow a plume of smoke in his eyes and he stares straight through it. This guy is tougher than concrete. But concrete can break.

'You'll regret that, Joe.'

I spin and roll, and there's the gun across the floor from me where Kieran dropped it. I grab it, muscle it, spin up and around and snap off a shot at Kieran, but he's gone.

'Time for some payback.' Kieran is right behind me. But he speaks before he acts, and I slam an elbow back and he grunts and doubles over.

'Do me a favour, smart guy,' I tell him. 'Try keeping your jaw closed.' And I pull back my fist for a sucker punch.

Then all hell breaks loose.

ONE HUNDRED AND NINE

The walls explode in on us and I duck and spin as screaming spiked stars come hurtling towards me. I take them down with a few well aimed shots. Through the debris I see Sue. Then something occurs to me.

'Take the watch off me, Kieran,' I shout, running for the cage. Behind me something growls and snarls and I don't even bother looking to see what it is, because the look on Sue's face tells me enough.

Kieran can't. There's something stopping him and I don't know what, but I don't intend to hang around long enough to find out.

The cage is shut, so as I race towards it I slam off a shot and the bullet sends the lock spinning into history. Sue's out like a flash with the Uzi in her hand and we're both running, as whatever is behind us snarls and growls.

'You can't get to him with bullets!' shouts Sue. 'You've got to think of a more intellectual way.'

'He can intellectualise my fist!' I yell, and suddenly there's a wall in front of us and it's getting bigger and bigger and there's no way around it.

Sue kicks in the Uzi and carves a circle of holes, roughly the size of the two of us, and we slam through and are out in the streets and into a living nightmare.

ONE HUNDRED AND TEN

Dante was right, but he just got the wrong location. The streets are filled with howling beasts and they've all got my number. A thousand deformed heads turn towards us, and we're off and running past the creatures. Jagged arms and heads with too many teeth reach out for us. They're quick, but we're quicker.

The way of the fist clears a path through the snarling, growling horde, with a smattering of assistance from the popgun and the Uzi.

Kieran looms up in the street ahead of us, his arms wide and his fingers splayed out. Lightning crackles in the air. It's all about to go wrong.

I pull up fast and stop Sue. The creatures behind us screech to a halt as Kieran looks at them. He's intrigued, confused, and as interested as anything else around us to see what I do next. And I don't even know myself.

'I'm starting to guess the problem, Kieran,' I say, stalling for time as I eye any exits. There are none. 'You can't take the watch from me. You might be able to screw around with the nature of reality—what moron can't?—but you can't take the watch. If you want co-operation from me you're going to have to start talking.'

'It's a deal.' Kieran's quick. No hesitation.

'Who was the monk? Where did he get the watch?'

'The watch has always been.' Kieran snaps his fingers and a whisky appears in his hand. One hovers in the air in front of me. I pass. 'The watch has always existed, a quick entrance into Hell. Dante was right in some ways, and so was everyone else. Hell used to be a cold, cold place, but now it's been commercialised. Whatever the demons dreamt up centuries ago was never enough for reality.'

Kieran laughs and there's compassion in his eyes, a yearning. I'm not buying it.

'We hate and we kill and we screw around with our lives and I want to change that.' There's anger now. That's more like it. 'I want to bring some order and justice to the underworld. I want to see the people who don't get any rights fight back against the system and get some recompense for a change. I don't want this reality to *be* this reality!'

'You become the system and they'll fight back against you,' I tell him. 'Save the speeches for the patsies who'll buy it. Why the watch? Why Hell? Who was the monk? That's all I'm asking.' I blow a plume of smoke in his face. 'For now.'

'Time for a history lesson,' says Kieran, and suddenly we're stuck in a dusty classroom wreathed in cobwebs. Kieran slams his hand against a chalkboard and dust puffs out. 'The watch has always been and always will be, passed on from person to person. Most people use and discard. Most people, like yourself, have no idea what kind of power they hold in their hands. Most people—'

'This is getting to be a speech, Kieran,' I say. 'Can it and move on to the facts.'

'The watch was never invented,' he tells us. 'It just exists, forever—no beginning and no end. The monk was one of the keepers of the watch, charged with making sure it didn't get in to the hands of mortals. Every few thousand years someone would come along and manage to acquire it—some people say with the monk's blessing—and use it as a gateway to the netherworld to check on the battle between good and evil. Or at least that's what the brochure said.'

Kieran stalks forward and faces me down.

'You managed to change things, Fury.' Kieran stares at me intently. 'You managed to change it. No one has ever done that before. You went into Hell and you ripped it a new one. You got Chicago in power and Bob, the true ruler of Hell, is a happy creature. Good and evil are no longer in conflict. That, my friend, is a very serious state of affairs.'

'You're still missing a question, smart guy,' I say. 'Why Hell? Why you?'

'Because the world as we know it will collapse and die without the eternal struggle *being* eternal. The metaphorical forces battling for the lives of man are no longer at war. If I can get into Hell, I can restore that disorder and continue the battle, and the world will not collapse. I can't get there by my own means, but the watch can take me there.'

'Sounds like a bunch of baloney.' I exhale smoke. 'What's in it for me?'

'You can rule by my side.'

'I'm not anyone's stooge,' I tell him. 'I work for myself and no one else. Give me something tangible.'

'Money?'

'I earn enough.'

'Power?'

'What would I need power for, Kieran?' I laugh at him and shake my head, scanning the room. No point running if this moron can change reality. 'It only leads to trouble.'

'Women?'

'I had a wife once,' I say. 'That's why I'm working double time. Try again.'

'Fame.'

'You're running out of options.' I stand up. 'Come up with something and we might be talking.'

'What do you want, Joe?' Kieran asks, lost. 'Just tell me.'

'I want to close this case, bring you in, and get on with my life.'

'Deal.' Kieran speaks before he thinks and I clap the cuffs on him with a smile.

'My pleasure,' I tell him.

'Rats,' he mutters, sinking his head. 'Rats and worms.'

'You're coming with me, tough guy.' I grab him by the collar and start marching him towards the door of the classroom, hoping the bluff works. Sue falls into step behind me. 'Preston might not want you, but we can stick you in the diner Chicago owns and something tells me you'll have trouble getting out. After all, that's his jurisdiction, not yours.'

'Rats and worms!' Kieran's voice is getting louder. 'Rats and worms! *Rats and worms!*'

I push him out of the door and into the dusty street. It should be an easy ride out of the zone, but Kieran's got his stooges waiting in one big wall right in front of us. All teeth, eyes and nasty smiles.

'Over there!' Sue jerks a thumb to a monster truck with a mini-gun on the back that's parked close by. I yank Kieran forward and we're off.

Sue jumps in the back and even before I'm in and gunning the engine she swings the mini-gun into action, tearing into the creatures as they surge forward.

'You'll never get out of here, Fury,' snarls Kieran.

'That's not the point,' I tell him, as we tear through the crowd and towards the main gates of the compound. 'I've got friends on the other side.'

'Chicago can't get in here!' shrieks Kieran. 'He's barred!'

'Whoever said it was Chicago.' And I wedge a grenade onto the accelerator and aim the truck for the compound gates.

'Now!' I yell to Sue, and she leaps out of the truck. I jump clear with Kieran in tow, and we hit the ground and roll. The monster truck slams into the compound gates and goes up in a blistering fireball, blowing creatures everywhere. The gates are torn in two, twisted steel flying.

Then the ninja chickens arrive.

ONE HUNDRED AND ELEVEN

It's one big mess of feathers and kung fu as they stream through the blasted compound gates. It starts with a scuffle and some clucking and suddenly Justice, the head chicken, is punching his way through the demonic mass followed by his league of chickens, all armed to the teeth and ready for action.

'Thought you might need some help,' he chuckles.

'How did you know where we are?' I yell.

'The fork Ginger gave you,' shouts Justice. 'It sent us a signal and led us to the compound. It wouldn't work unless it was close to Kieran. He might think he runs reality, but there's been plenty of people plotting his downfall for a long time now!'

'You can't get in here!' screams Kieran. 'It's impossible!'

Justice snaps him a glance. 'Time to meet your maker.'

'I *am* my maker!' shouts Kieran, and he rips himself out of my grip. Suddenly he's swamped by the crowd of demons and creatures and flying feathers.

'He won't get far.' Justice takes a step forward and then stops. 'Oh crap!'

Kieran's doubling in size with each step, sucking in everything around him. Parts of buildings tear towards him and slam into his body, and he ripples and mutates and grows.

People and chickens try to run, but his force draws them closer and sucks them in. His body bulges and juts out with arms and heads and legs. And they're all screaming.

Justice takes another step towards him but it's too late.

Kieran spins and flexes, his massive hands balled into fists. *'I am my maker!'* he screams again, as the forces of Hell explode into the compound.

ONE HUNDRED AND TWELVE

Justice and his league of ninja chickens steel themselves. This is going to be a tough one.

Kieran lets out an unearthly shriek and his minions—those that aren't part of him—come streaming out of the buildings. The two sides engage and the ground shakes. Justice takes a step towards Kieran and Kieran takes a step towards Justice and the two clash in a thunderous roar.

Justice right hooks him, but Kieran's a dirty fighter. The heads in his torso start to bite, and Justice feels it. He crashes down a wing and crushes a few heads, the craniums popping. Kieran slams razor sharp fingernails into Justice's side and starts to tear downwards, ripping him open.

Justice staggers back, gasping, and swings for Kieran, but Kieran catches his wing and crushes his feathers. It's not looking good.

Sue jacks back the slide on the Uzi, but there's no clear shot. 'Damn.'

'Kieran's stronger than all of us,' I say. 'We need something drastic.' And a legion of zombies burst into the fray from the outside world.

Justice jabs a wing tip at Kieran. 'Zombies! Attack!' They do, streaming over the ground towards him, swarming up his legs and tearing solid chunks out of his skin. But the more of him they remove, the more he sucks in his followers, building in mass and size as he crushes Justice's wing. He roars in victory and fury, heaving Justice into the air.

Justice uses his other wing to kung fu a breather for himself, and falls down beside us in a mass of feathers. But he's not ready for the hot pot yet.

'That's not helping,' I yell to Justice. 'We need something bigger.'

'It's just a temporary diversion,' he shouts back. 'Something to slow him down so we can use this.' He turns, pointing to a giant helicopter gun ship which lands behind us. 'Time for the big guns.' And I swear there's a smile on his beak.

ONE HUNDRED AND THIRTEEN

We're in and up, Justice at the controls. Sue swings out the machine gun and I just smoke and take it easy.

'This has been coming for a long time,' says Justice, and he sweeps the gun ship round and starts firing, tearing rockets into Kieran's head. The side of his skull explodes and he staggers sideways.

Justice pulls the gun ship around for another go and bullets rake across Kieran's body. He swipes for us, but Justice is too quick, ripping the gun ship into a tight turn, the hand missing by inches. Justice spins the helicopter around and lets loose another flurry of missiles. They tear into Kieran, blowing chunks out of his deformed chest, ripping him open. But more bodies slam into him as he loses parts. He buckles and stands up again, and he's twice the size he was before.

'We need something more serious!' I yell at Justice. A brace of tanks smash through the fighting hordes and head straight for Kieran, guns blazing.

The shells explode into him and knock him back. Fighter jets and more gun ships stream out of the sky. Now everyone's firing, missiles and shells pouring in towards Kieran as he ripples and mutates and tries to fight back against us. The over-whelming firepower knocks Kieran back and down, but people are still getting sucked into him, and the world is filled with the sound of the masses screaming.

'It's working!' Justice goes in for the kill and there's so much smoke and fire that Kieran gets lost in it. We stream through and see something large and ungainly thrashing, but it's just a vague figure.

Justice pulls up and we wait for the smoke to clear. It doesn't take long. And Kieran's not there. There's a lot of blood and a hole in the ground.

'He's gone underground.' Justice sets the gun ship down. 'He can't stay there for long.'

A giant arm bursts out of the ground and picks up one of the tanks, crushing it. Metal buckles and the shells inside the tank explode in a raging fireball, but the hand is unmarked.

'Scramble!' Justice shrieks into the headset. He tries to take off, but the hand slams into us and knocks us spinning.

ONE HUNDRED AND FOURTEEN

The 'copter crashes into the ground and sheds the three of us like an old skin. I'm up with the cannon out and over to Sue.

'You okay?'

She nods, whips out her Uzi and looks very pissed off. 'It's time for some personal payback.'

The jets stream missiles at the ground, but Kieran's giant fist punches through the earth and takes them out, crushing them in a blossoming fireball. The fingers of the hand uncurl and blot out the sun, then the hand slams down towards us.

I start popping off shots and Sue rakes the Uzi left and right, punching bloody holes in the skin, but it's too big and too tough for us.

Justice steps out of the wreckage with a rocket launcher. He kneels, fires, and sends a missile hurtling towards the hand, blowing off one of the fingers. But it's not enough.

I fire round after round into the hand, then I whip out the watch. 'Let's negotiate.'

The hand stops, inches from our heads. The mist swirls around us and Kieran's standing there, good as new, normal size, brushing flecks of dirt off his clothes and looking smug, surrounded by a wall of fire, wreckage and body parts.

'So you decided to see sense?' he says.

'I don't have a choice.' I snap open a pack of cigars and spark one up, drawing the smoke in deep. 'You're proving to be a bit of a problem.'

'Only for those who cause me trouble.' Kieran snaps his fingers and suddenly we're sitting in leather chairs. The wreckage still burns around us, but at least it's more comfortable.

'You see what I can do with reality?' Kieran looks pleased with himself. 'You see why I need to take over Hell and bring some order to it?'

'Yeah, you're keeping this place looking peachy,' I sneer. 'What do I get in return for the watch?'

'You don't want power, fame, money or women. What do you want?'

'I want an endless bottle of whisky, a pack of Havanas that never runs out, a tank of gas which never empties for my shark, and a bit of peace and quiet around this joint. That's the deal.'

Kieran pauses for a moment and then nods. 'Certainly.'

I hold up the watch. 'And I don't want to see your ugly face around my patch any more, capiche?'

'Of course.'

'You can have it.'

Justice runs forward. 'Fury, no!'

'I don't have a choice,' I tell him, and move the watch towards Kieran. He hesitates, uncertain of the power, then smiles and puts his hand out. I drop the watch in.

'It's mine,' he gloats. 'All mine.'

'Just one more question,' I say.

'Fire away.'

'Why couldn't you just take it off me?'

'The watch has to be handed over willingly, or else the recipient dies,' says Kieran.

I stand up and move over to Sue. Kieran smiles at us, and his look turns evil.

'I'm afraid we have a problem, Mr Fury.' Kieran sits back, twirling the watch in his fingers. 'I lied.'

'I figured as much.'

'Now there is no end to what I can do. Now the world and

the heavens and Hell will all bow down to me. Now I will rule the very nature of reality.'

'Nice speech,' I mutter, puffing on the cigar and pulling out the cannon. 'Now let's see if you can outsmart this bullet.'

Sue snatches a look at me and I nod.

And everything switches into slow motion.

Kieran's finger comes down on the stop watch just as I pull the trigger.

The bullet explodes from the barrel of the cannon in a stream of sparks and smoke and sails towards the watch.

The instant Kieran's finger clicks the button the bullet smashes the watch.

And time.

Crawls.

To a stop.

Kieran doesn't even have time to scream before he disappears.

And it's over.

ONE HUNDRED AND FIFTEEN

Justice wanders over to me as I re-light the Havana. 'What happened?' he asks.

'Kieran won't be messing around with reality anymore,' I tell him. 'He's trapped in time. Forever. Frozen. He can't fix the watch, so he's stuck in Hell with Chicago's boys, unable to move. At least, that's what I figure.'

Justice stares at Sue. 'You peachy?'

'Bruised and branded,' says Sue. 'But I'll live.'

Justice turns to me. 'See you on the flip side, private eye.'

'The pleasure's all mine.' I give him a nod and he ambles off towards the clucking ninja chicken hordes that make up his clan.

I turn to Sue. 'Got any plans?'

'I need a drink,' she says.

I pull a small whisky bottle from my coat and throw it over. 'Indulge yourself.'

She smiles and takes a hit, then throws it back. 'That was some trick with the watch.'

'Let's hope I'm right.'

She looks at me for a second, then—'You're one tough cookie.'

'I know.'

She smiles, and we walk off through the wreckage and fire.

ONE HUNDRED AND SIXTEEN

I'm sitting in the office with Sue when the door opens and Chicago walks in.

'It's been a while,' he says, taking a seat. 'Thought you might want to know the news.'

'What have you got?'

'You were right about Kieran,' says Chicago. 'Caught in time, frozen in Hell. My boys took him apart as soon as he appeared. Took seconds.'

'And the watch?'

'Shattered,' says Chicago. 'Useless. And the end of an era.'

'That's good to know.' I nod and settle back. 'Anything else I can do for you?'

Chicago shifts uncomfortably. 'Well, there is a small problem in Hell at the moment. It's a bit of a delicate matter. I was wondering if you can help.'

'That's what I'm here for,' I say, and we start the ball rolling again.

ACKNOWLEDGEMENTS

First of all, love, admiration and thanks to Hazel Maria Humphreys for all her hard work, help, dedication, belief and suffrage in the lifespan of this book and beyond, amongst many other things.

Thanks to Dan Lacey for years of friendship and beers. But mainly the beers.

Thanks to Rob Franklin and Charlotte Batten for their help, Rob Dwyer and Steve Hampton and the Old Boy's Network for giving me an opportunity to film with them, Tina Severe for the logo, Ed Jordan for his camerawork, Will Franklin for his fantastic acting, Aaron Harding for his bald spot, Martyn Threader for being so short, Georgina Martin for hiring me as editor, Jon and Amanda, Trev and Mel, Steve and Gail and Leigh and Jane, Jacko for the name 'Ironballs', Marsha for kicking my arse on Soul Calibur, Steve Hammal, Glen Maney, Rick and Joe Barbs and many others too numerous to mention—if I missed you out blame someone else.

Lightning Source UK Ltd.
Milton Keynes UK
02 September 2009

143297UK00001B/16/P

9 781843 501053